Strange Fruit

Strange Fruit

Bryan David Hiltner

VANTAGE Press
New York

This is a work of fiction. Any similarity between the names
and characters in this book and any real persons, living or
dead, is purely coincidental.

Cover design by Susan Thomas

Vantage Press and the Vantage Press colophon
are registered trademarks of Vantage Press, Inc.

FIRST EDITION

Published by Vantage Press, Inc.
419 Park Ave. South, New York, NY 10016

Manufactured in the United States of America
ISBN: 978-0-533-15726-6

Library of Congress Catalog Card No.: 2007900281

0 9 8 7 6 5 4 3 2 1

Strange Fruit

One

It was a hot day when we arrived in Miner's Bluff in the state of Georgia. My partner and I had been sent by the Federal Bureau of Investigation to look into a lynching that occurred here within the past few months. This was a special one involving a young Negro boy named Nathaniel. Nathaniel Johnson. He was only twelve. The nature and the brutality of his death was indescribable. He was only a child. We needed and wanted answers and we came here to get them.

We arrived at one of the worst possible times. It was one of the hottest summers on record. The temperature must have been about 110 degrees in the shade. The summer of 1963 would get even hotter. We had made our way there from our offices in Atlanta. I came down from D.C. My soon-to-be partner was already working in Atlanta. The FBI in D.C. thought it would be a good idea to team me up with someone familiar with the people and the countryside where we would be going.

Both of us made our way by car, driving about forty-five miles west of Atlanta towards Miner's Bluff. The town was about five miles from the Alabama border. It was a small town, maybe about a thousand people live there. A majority of the people who lived in Miner's Bluff were Negroes. The others were white. The Negroes lived on the outskirts of the town. What they lived in I wouldn't call houses. More like shacks. They were very poor and so far had lived horrible lives. The whites, on the other hand, lived in very nice

1

houses with white picket fences and seemed to be living a good life. Pretty soon that would all change.

It was not a particularly good time to be a government man as they say down here, especially if you were investigating something. The south was not too happy having the likes of me and my partner there. The civil rights movement was becoming stronger every day. The south was feeling it more than any other part of the country. They felt their very existence was at stake and they would do anything, and everything, to stop it—even murder.

I had heard and seen things from other investigators sent to other southern states like Mississippi and Alabama: the murder of innocent men, women and children; the bombing of churches and homes. All because a group of people wanted the same rights as their white counterparts. Now we were in Georgia. It was going to be one of my hardest assignments ever.

About to get out of the car, I thought, *How are these people going to react to me? I have a feeling a lot of questions are going to be unanswered.*

I opened the car door, but before I got out, I turned to my partner and told him, "Stay put. I'm about to go and see the sheriff of the town and I don't think it's a good idea if you come with me."

He looked at me and said, "Hell no! I'm not waiting here in this car by myself."

I looked at him, shook my head, and said, "Fine, come on, but you know what they're going to say to you."

We both got out and started across the street. Several people sitting outside of the stores watched us as we made our way across the street.

Suddenly a car came flying down the street at a high rate of speed heading right towards us. It came straight at my partner and I had to pull him out of the way. It was no accident. The driver meant to hit us. As he went by, he honked his horn. I saw the people sitting there smiling. Things were off to a bad start already.

I walked into the sheriff's office. A deputy was sitting behind a desk sideways with his feet on the desk and talking to someone on the phone.

I said very politely, "Excuse me, Deputy. My name is Agent Daniel Pierce, this is my partner Agent Franklin Jones. I'm here to see Sheriff Crawford."

The deputy continued to talk on the phone. I asked him again very nicely, "Can I see Sheriff Crawford?" He kept on talking.

I looked at my partner and he looked at me. I then walked over to where the deputy sat. Using my hands, I forcibly pushed his feet off the desk and then grabbed him by his shirt collar.

He looked at me with a startled look as I proceeded to ask him again, "Can I see Sheriff Crawford?"

He said to the person on the phone, "I have to go. I'll call you back." He then hung up.

I asked the deputy, "What's your name?"

He said, "My name is Henry, Henry Shamus. People around here call me 'Hank.' "

I said, "Well, Hank, I need to see the sheriff right away."

Hank said, "Well, I don't know if I can arrange that right now. You see the sheriff is a very busy person and he doesn't like being disturbed if it's not important business."

I started to get angry. *How thick could he be?* I moved closer to his face. We were about eye to eye when I said, "Apparently you don't know who or what I am. You see, I work for the government. I'm with the FBI. You work for the government. So that means we both work for the government. Are you understanding me now?"

I let go of his collar and walked back around the desk.

He looked at me and said, "I'll see if he is able to see you, but not your partner."

I asked him, "Why?"

He said. "The sheriff doesn't talk to no nig . . ." He stopped in mid-sentence.

Agent Jones had a crooked smile on his face. He said to the deputy, "Go ahead finish what you were going to say. The sheriff doesn't want to talk to a nigger. Isn't that what you were about to say?"

I turned to Agent Jones and said, "Not now, please."

Deputy Hank got up from his desk and headed for the sheriff's door. He turned to me and said, "Wait here and I'll see if he's able to see you."

I turned to Agent Jones and said, "You have to not let these people bother you. I know it's going to be hard. We were sent here to investigate a crime, not to start a race war. You know I am on your side." Agent Jones shook his head from side to side and let out a sigh.

A few minutes had passed since the deputy went into the sheriff's office and I was getting a little angry. *What's going on here? I'll give him another minute.*

I was about to storm into the office when suddenly the door opened and the deputy walked out. Right behind him was a short, burly-looking man with an unlit cigar stuck in his mouth. He walked towards me and stopped about a foot away.

"My deputy here said you want to talk to me about something," he said with a thick southern drawl. He continued, "I can't possibly know what you government guys would want to talk to me about."

I thought *Oh great, he's going to play stupid. This is going to be fun.*

"Well, Sheriff, we were sent here by the American government to find out about the unexplained murder of a young Negro boy down here in Miner's Bluff."

He took the cigar out of his mouth and said, "I don't know what you are talking about."

I began to press him hard. "I know for a fact that you know all about what happened here. Trying to use ignorance is not going to help you."

I pulled a bunch of papers out of my briefcase and threw them on the sheriff's desk. I said to him, "Are you going to tell me you don't know anything about any murder that happened in your own town? I really find that hard to believe."

He shook his head and started to chuckle. His mood seemed to change quickly. "You government boys from the north, you think you can come down here and accuse us of things you don't even know about. Why don't you get back in your little black car and go home before you get hurt."

I knew it wasn't going to be easy, but I was not about to back down. We had been sent for a reason and we were not going to leave until all our questions had been answered. I didn't care how long it took.

I got real close to his face and said, "Is that a threat, Sheriff? If it is and anything happens to me or my partner, the government will have a few hundred agents coming to your town and turning it upside down."

He chuckled again. I turned to Agent Jones and said, "Let's go." I then turned back around and said, "Sheriff Crawford, I'm going to be here for a long time. I'll be back sometime to see you again and you're not going to be happy about it.

Agent Jones and I walked back to our car. As we neared the car, I saw that the front tire was flat. One of the friendly townsfolk must have let the air out.

I popped open the trunk and removed the spare tire and jack. As bad as it was, it could have been worse. They could have flattened all the tires. Agent Jones and I changed the tire as quickly as possible. It would be dark soon and I didn't want to still be there when it was.

We needed a place to stay and I thought it best to drive out of the town to look for a motel instead of one in town. Anyway, I didn't think they would appreciate a white and a black man sharing a room. I started to drive out of town. After some time I decided to turn down a dirt road. I noticed a car was following us.

I turned to Agent Jones and said, "I don't like this one bit. There is someone following us."

He turned around very slowly and looked out the rear window. He turned and looked at me and said, "Oh, shit, you're right." I saw the panic on Agent Jones' face. He knew what it was like. He'd been through it before.

I slowed down and then pulled over to the side of the road. In my rearview mirror I saw the car slow down too. I got out of the car and walked around it. I acted like I was looking at the tire. I bent down next to the tire and started to fiddle with it while at the same time I looked in the direction of the car. It was coming closer and then suddenly it passed us. I stood and looked constantly at the car. It continued down the road and disappeared beyond the horizon.

I got back into the car. Agent Jones and I both let out a sigh of relief. Our job would not be easy and darkness would be our enemy.

I started to drive very slowly. Both of us were on guard. Agent Jones constantly scanned our surroundings. We didn't know if we would be ambushed.

We were finally out of town. I drove for a couple of miles when not too far in the distance, I saw flashing lights of a motel on the roadside. I drove towards it. It didn't look like much, but I didn't care. I was tired and we needed a place to stay. I pulled into the parking lot.

I told Agent Jones, "Stay in the car."

He was not happy about it and said, "Are you going to be saying that to me the whole time we are down here, 'stay in the car'?"

I turned to him and said, "Would you like to go in there and get a room for us? I'm sure you'll have no problem getting us one. I would be happy to let you go, but apparently you don't realize where we are at."

He just smiled and said, "I'll wait in the car. Don't be long, this place scares the shit out of me."

I walked into the motel lobby. The gentleman who stood behind the counter looked like he hadn't taken a bath in a few weeks. I walked over to the counter. He asked, "Can I help you, mister?"

I said, "Yes, I need a room for the night. Preferably one that has a bathroom and shower."

He replied, "All our rooms have bathrooms and a shower. They don't have TVs. Wait, are you trying to be funny?"

I said, "No. I apologize if it came out that way."

He gave me a look, then rose and got the key to the room. He said, "That will be ten dollars a day and I only accept cash." He looked me up and down. "You seem a little overdressed for these parts. Are you a some kind of businessman from up north?"

I smiled, shook my head, and said, "You found me out. Yes, I am a businessman from the north. I come from Ohio. I'm thinking of opening my business down here. I make cogs for clocks."

He nodded his head and said, "That's nice, we need some jobs down here."

I went back to the car. I told Agent Jones, "Get down in the seat."

He said, "Why? For what reason?"

I said back, "Agent Jones, our wonderful innkeeper thinks it's only me who is staying here. I don't think he would have rented the motel room to me if he knew I had a black person with me. Is that a good enough reason?"

Agent Jones ducked down as I drove to our room. Thankfully it was all the way down at the end of the building and pretty much out of sight.

Luckily it was dark so Agent Jones could sneak into the room. I opened the door. It wasn't much. I'd seen better rooms in condemned buildings, but it would do. It had two small beds.

I asked Agent Jones, "Which one of the beds do you want?"

He said, "I don't care. I'm just tired and want to get some sleep."

I went back outside and brought our luggage in. I got out clothes to wear the next day and put them to the side.

I was still a little sticky and sweaty from the heat of the day, so I told Agent Jones, "I'm going to take a cold shower."

He was already flat out on his bed. I walked into the bathroom. It wasn't very clean. I turned on the water. It didn't come out very fast. I stuck my head under it.

I thought, *What am I getting myself into? What was the agency thinking when they teamed me up with a black man? Do they know how hard it's going to be to get anything out of these people with him here? What the hell were they thinking?*

I had my head under the shower for at least ten minutes before I turned off the water and started to dry off. I thought about out plans for the next day.

We need to get out and speak to some of the people, especially black people. We need to talk to them. They are going to be the key to uncovering whatever happened here.

I came out of the bathroom and saw Agent Jones was fast asleep. I tried to creep around quietly so as not to wake him. I decided to wear only a pair of boxer shorts and no shirt. It was god-awful hot in the room and there was no air-conditioning. My cold shower turned out to be useless.

I wasn't very tired, so I decided to clean my gun. I didn't know if I would ever need it, but I wanted to make sure it worked if I did. It only took me a few minutes. Since there was no television, there wasn't much else to do except read the Bible. Since I wasn't tired I decided to read it. I thought it would surely put me to sleep.

The next thing I knew it was morning. I heard the birds chirping. It was hot, so we had left the windows open. Agent Jones was still asleep. He seemed to be quite the sleeper. Even the heat and mosquitoes didn't bother him. I looked at my watch. It was 5:45.

I walked over to Agent Jones' bed and shook it took wake him. He just turned over to the other side. I shook it again and yelled at him.

Suddenly, his eyes were wide open and he said, "Don't yell, I'm awake." He then proceeded to put his head back down on the pillow. I grabbed his legs and yanked him off the bed onto the floor.

He walked to the shower and closed the door. After a couple of minutes, I heard him singing to himself. I couldn't tell what he was singing. I went got dressed and went about getting everything ready for our day. I pulled out a notepad to write names, addresses, or any information pertaining to the investigation.

Most of the people we were going to talk to would be black. I thought, *I wonder if they will talk to us. Most are scared to death to speak to anyone. What will they be willing to tell us?*

Suddenly, the bathroom door flew open and Agent Jones came out stark naked humming to himself.

I asked him, "From now on, if you would please wear a towel around yourself when coming out of the bathroom."

He looked at me, laughed, and said, "What are you jealous?"

I said, "No, I just don't get any enjoyment looking at a nude body of a man."

We had to get on our way. There was a lot of investigating to do and we needed to get it done as soon as possible in order to get out of there alive. I decided we needed to speak to the murdered boy's grandmother. I had a feeling it would be hard for her to talk about it. Even so, she needed to tell us everything she knew.

Her home was just within the city limits We had to drive down an unpaved road. As we did, dirt and dust kicked up and I could barely see in front of us. We must have gone about a quarter mile down the road. There were a few houses, if you could call them that, on both sides of the road. I needed to find one that was painted red. I drove a little farther and saw it on the right side of the road. I parked in front of a fallen down fence.

Agent Jones and I got out of the car and walked towards the house. We needed to step over the fence. As Agent Jones stepped over it, he caught the bottom of his left pant leg on a piece of fence that was sticking up. He nearly tumbled to the ground, but caught his balance. He ended up tearing his pant leg and, of course, he started to curse.

The grass in the yard was waist high. It probably hadn't been cut in years. We stepped very carefully as we walked towards the door since we didn't know what we were stepping in or on.

I knocked on the door. I waited a few minutes for an answer. I looked around as we waited. I saw some older black people sitting on their porches. I guess they were checking us out and probably wondering who the guys in black suits were, especially since one was black and the other white.

I decided to knock again. I knocked a little harder. Suddenly, the door creaked open a little bit. I saw someone peering out from the slit. When I started to introduce myself and Agent Jones, the door opened a little more. I saw a small face peering out. It looked like a little girl. The door opened even more. In full view of me was a little black girl, who looked to be about seven or eight.

She stared up at me, I asked her, "Little girl, is your grandmother home?"

She looked at me for a few seconds and then said, "Yeah."

I continued, "Can I see your grandmother?"

She said, "Wait here, I'll see if she wants to see you."

Agent Jones and I waited for the girl to return. The sun was shining down hard and it was hot as hell. I needed to get in the shade pretty quick or I would pass out.

The little girl came back and said, "My grandmamma said, 'Who are you?' "

I told the little girl, "We are from the government and we want to ask her a few questions."

The girl left again. We waited a few more minutes. I was getting tired of it and was about to leave when the little girl came back again.

She said, "C'mon in, I'll take you to her."

We followed the girl. The house was poorly lit. It didn't appear there were any lights in the house at all. There was hardly any furniture. As we walked, the floorboards creaked very loudly. I felt like I was going to fall through them at any moment. The house had sort of a musty smell.

The little girl took us to a back room. Sitting at an old beat-up table was her grandmother, Nathaniel's grandmother. She was an elderly woman with white hair that was combed back. She wore a sleeveless housedress. I could tell by her mouth that she didn't have any teeth.

I walked over and introduced myself and Agent Jones. I

said, "Mrs. Johnson, I'm Agent Pierce and this is Agent Jones. We're from the FBI. We're investigating your grandson's death. We need to get some information. I hope you can answer a few questions."

She looked both of us up and down. I guess she was wondering what we were all about and why were we there. It was extremely hot inside the house even as dark as it was. I pulled out a handkerchief from my pocket and wiped my brow.

Mrs. Johnson smiled. "It gets awful hot down here, don't it?"

I nodded my head.

She called to her granddaughter, "Ruby, c'mon back in here a minute."

Ruby said, "Yes, Grandmamma. What do you want?"

Mrs. Johnson said, "Ruby, why don't you get somethin' for these gentlemen to drink."

Ruby asked us, "What you want to drink?"

I told her, "Water will be fine."

Agent Jones said, "The same."

Mrs. Johnson said, "No water for them, Ruby, get them a glass of lemonade I just made."

I said, "Lemonade it is." I tried to steer the conversation back to her grandson. "Mrs. Johnson, could you tell us about the night when your grandson died? Do you remember what happened exactly?"

Mrs. Johnson replied, "I try not to think about that. It just brings back a lot of sorrow and bad memories."

I said to her, "We're here to help you, Mrs. Johnson. My partner and I want justice for your grandson, but we're going to need your help."

She started to cry a little and looked around the room. "Let me tell you something, sir, there is no justice down here.

It's been happening for the last hundred years and ain't nothin' goin' to change that."

I grabbed her hand that was on the table and said to her, "I know it's hard to trust anyone right now, especially someone white, but I'm telling you this time, it's going to be different. We're not leaving until we know the truth and the person or people who did this are behind bars."

I thought pleading with her might loosen her up. It wasn't working. I asked her again.

She said, "I lived a long life, it don't matter what happens to me. I'm worried about my other children and grandchildren. If I say anything, they are going to come after all of us for sure and they will kill us."

We both walked out to the front yard. Agent Jones turned to me and said, "Let me talk to her alone. I think she doesn't trust anybody white. She might talk to me. It can't hurt to let me try talking to her."

I decided to light as cigarette and started smoking it. We needed to know what she knew. Her testimony was crucial for the case. I paced back and forth in the yard. I threw the cigarette on the ground and stamped it out with my shoe.

I turned to Agent Jones and said, "Go ahead. Try to get as much information as you can. Take a pad and pencil and write down every detail you get out of her."

Agent Jones went back into the house. I decided to do some investigating of my own. I threw my jacket in the back seat of the car and then I walked over to another house. An elderly black gentleman sat in an old rocking chair on the porch. The sun was shining so brightly that I had to put my hand over my eyes to see him.

I stood in the road and called to him. "Excuse me, sir, I'd like to talk to you for minute if I can." He just stared at me. I repeated what I said.

He got up from the rocking chair and waved to me to come in. I walked the path to the front porch and up a few steps. I introduced myself and put my hand out to shake his. He looked at my hand for a few seconds and slowly took my hand and shook it. I guess he hadn't shaken a lot of white men's hands while living there.

I asked him, "What's your name?"

He said, "It's George and that's all you'll get for my name."

I smiled and said, "That's fine. I'm investigating the death of Nathaniel Johnson."

He looked up at me and said, "I don't know nothin' about that. I didn't see nothin'. I didn't hear nothin'."

I knew immediately I wasn't going to get much information out of him or anybody else for that matter.

I decided to walk back to the Johnson house. I pulled out another cigarette and lit it. I leaned against the car and waited for Agent Jones to come out. I waited for about ten minutes when suddenly he walked out the door. I got up from leaning against the car.

I asked him, "So what did she tell you?"

He looked at me with a depressed look on his face. He said, "Not that much."

This was great. How are we going to get anything if no one is willing to talk to us? Even the grandmother.

We both got in the car. I continued asking questions about what she said. Agent Jones gave me some information.

"This is what she told me," Agent Jones said. "She said that supposedly her grandson made a pass at this little white girl. Some of the white men of the town found out about it. They found out where he lived and came to get him. While he was not too far from home, they grabbed him. He started to scream and struggle and was yelling for his grandmother.

Mrs. Johnson came out and saw them throw him in the back seat of a car. That's the only thing she remembers."

I asked, "Did she see how many men there were or what was the color or make of the car that these men were in?"

He said, "She saw three, but couldn't tell me what they looked like. She couldn't tell what kind of car it was or what color it was. She said it was too dark out. That's all the information I could get out of her."

It wasn't much, but it was something. If she could have told us about the car, it would have helped a lot. The fear of reprisal in town hurt our investigation. No one was willing to talk to us for fear of something happening to them. It was a scary thing.

We had a somewhat productive day, but there was still plenty of investigating to do. I decided it was time to return to the motel. Agent Jones was hungry and wanted something to eat before we went back, so I drove toward the center of town. I thought we could get a bite to eat at one of the restaurants there.

I decided to stop at the first one I saw. I parked in front of it. Agent Jones and I walked into the restaurant. Suddenly, everyone inside turned towards us to look. Their facial expressions were a little disturbing.

A young waitress rushed toward us and stood in front of me. She said, "You're going to have to leave, mister."

I looked at her strangely and asked her, "Why?"

She replied, "I'm sorry, but we don't serve no Negroes here. So you're going to have to leave."

I started to become angry. I didn't understand why. For a moment I had forgotten I was in the South. I told her, "No, I want to be seated and served."

She came even closer to me and whispered to me, "Look, mister, I don't want no trouble. If I have to, I'm going to call the police."

15

I said, "Fine." I proceeded to pull out my badge and show her it. "You see, Miss, I'm sort of like the police too. I work for the FBI. That's part of the government."

Just then Agent Jones grabbed my arm. He leaned over to me and said in my one ear, "Let's just go. I don't want this to turn into a brawl." We turned around and walked out the door.

I turned to Agent Jones and said, "Why did you do that? We work for the government. They can't threaten us."

Agent Jones said nothing.

We had to look for another place to eat. Agent Jones just stared out the windshield of the car. He turned to me and said, "You don't understand how it is down here. There is only black and white. There is no gray, no middle ground. The races don't mix down here like they do in the north. You are going to have to understand that. If not, we're going to run into a lot of problems."

I decided to drive back to the motel, let Agent Jones out, and then go looking for someplace to get some food. When I dropped him, I said, "Go in and lock the door and do not let anyone in unless you know it's me."

He said, "Don't worry, I can take care of myself. I've had to deal with this all my life."

I spun off in search of food. I wanted to get back before dark. It was a pretty dangerous place during the day, but a hundred times worse at night. I needed to always be on guard. As I drove around, I constantly looked around. Looking in my rearview mirror, I wondered if someone might try to run me off the road or even worse, try to kill me.

I came across a small store. I parked and went inside. An elderly woman was behind the counter. I walked passed her and said, "Hello."

I proceeded to walk around the store, looking for items that I could take back to the motel. I picked up a big bag of

16

potato chips. I then came across loaves of bread and picked one up. *Maybe I can find some kind of meat to make sandwiches out of.*

I went to the counter and asked the woman behind it, "Do you have any kind of luncheon meat?"

She pointed over to a small freezer, which I opened. There were packages of luncheon meats inside. I picked up something that looked like pimento loaf. I really didn't like pimento loaf, but I was hungry and we needed to eat something. I looked for cheese and found some in another freezer. All I needed was something to drink. There were some bottles of root beer soda sitting next to the freezer. I picked up a couple bottles and headed to the counter.

I put my items on the counter. The woman started to pick them up. She looked at them and then looked at me. She entered the amount of the items into the register. She said, "I've never seen you before. You new in town?"

I smiled and just said, "Yes, I am." She continued to ask questions and I just smiled at her. Finally, I said, "I'm really in a hurry, could you speed it up a little?"

I think she was annoyed at what I said and she stopped asking questions. She turned to me with a irate expression and said, "That will be three dollars and fifty-nine cents, mister."

I pulled out a five, gave it to her, and said, "You can keep the change." I wanted to get out of there as soon as possible.

I hopped into the car and started back to the motel. It was getting dark and I needed to get back. I flew down the road as fast as possible. It felt like I was being followed. *Did that woman tell someone about me?* I looked in the rearview mirror and saw car headlights in the distance. I decided to speed up.

Finally back at the motel, I looked back again but didn't see the headlights anymore. I hoped I hadn't been followed.

I got out of the car and walked to the door. I knocked hard and saw Agent Jones peer out from behind the curtains. *Good, he listened to what I told him.*

The door finally opened. I walked over to the table in the room and put the bag down on it.

Agent Jones said, "I'm glad you're back, I'm starving. What did you get?" I told him what I brought back. He said, "Pimento loaf. I don't know if I ever had that. I'm so hungry I could eat a pig's scrotum."

I thought, *Now that's appealing.*

I opened the loaf of bread and put a slice of pimento loaf and cheese on the slices of bread and handed it to Agent Jones.

He said, "What, no mustard?" He chuckled.

We started to eat our sandwiches. It wasn't the greatest dinner in the world, but it was something to eat.

I sat on my bed and Agent Jones on his while we ate. After we were finished, I started to talk about the case.

I told him, "We need to interview more people. I've gotten some more leads and there are some people in town I want to speak to. Some white, some black."

I was still going on about the case when Agent Jones interrupted me. "Don't you ever think of anything but the case?"

I was surprised by his statement and sort of offended. *We are FBI agents. We were sent here to try and solve a murder, that's why we are here. What am I supposed to talk about, the weather, maybe baseball?*

I asked him, "What do you expect me to talk about? I don't know if you remember, but we are working on a case right now."

He said, "I know that, but does it have to be non-stop, twenty-four hours a day? Maybe we could talk about the weather or something else."

I said to him, "Maybe this case is too much for you. If you don't want to continue, I can get someone to replace you. I'll call the field office in Atlanta tomorrow."

He replied angrily, "That's not what I'm saying. You have a life, I have a life. There's more to what we are than this case. Do we always have to be on the clock? Can't we just relax and have a nice talk?"

I aid, "Fine, what do you want to talk about?"

He said, "Not the case, that's for damn sure." He continued, "I don't even know that much about you. Where you live, if you're married, do you have any children?"

I wondered, *Why does he need to know all this? What does this have to do with why we're here?*

He wanted to talk, so I talked. I told him, "I was born in Buffalo, New York. My father was a police officer, my mother was a housewife. I went to college at the University of Rochester and studied criminal law. I decided to go into law enforcement and then I decided I wanted to be a FBI agent. I've never been married. I have no children that I know of. Are you happy now?"

Agent Jones shook his head and laughed. "Well, I guess I expected that kind of answer from you. A nice and tidy clinical answer. Straight to the point."

I said to him, "Well, tell me about yourself."

Agent Jones started "All right, I will. I was born here in Georgia. I stayed here until I was eight. My mother decided to send me up to live in Chicago with my aunt. My mother had seven kids to take care of. I was the only boy. She thought it would be better if I lived with my aunt. I would have a better life. You see the life expectancy of a male Negro is not very long down here." He stopped suddenly.

I said, "Continue."

He said, "Are you sure you want to hear all this?"

I nodded my head.

He continued, "I was sent up right after my father died when I was young It was hard being a young Negro boy in the South. The North seemed to be more tolerant of black folks than the South. Or so I thought. It was just as bad. But I always hated the South and the white people that lived here and for what they stood for. Eventually, I got over it."

Agent Jones stopped again. He got up and walked over to the window. He looked out, just staring. I left him alone for a few minutes. I didn't want to push him. I wanted to know more, but I didn't want him to get upset. I waited until he wanted to tell me more.

He turned around, walked over to his bed, and sat on the end of it. He started to talk again. "I'm sorry about this."

I told him, "It's all right. Are you married or have any children?"

He said, "Yeah, I'm married. I have two small children. A girl and a boy."

He reached into his pants pocket and pulled out his wallet. He took a picture out. He got up and handed it to me.

He said, "That's my wife Dorothy. The little girl is Jamela, she's four years old. The boy's name is Franklin, Junior, he's six."

I looked at the picture and smiled. I then handed it back to Agent Jones and said, "You have a beautiful family, you should be very proud."

He smiled back and said,"I am very proud of them."

Agent Jones then asked, "Are you ever going to get married?

I said, "I don't know, well, not yet. I guess I haven't found the right woman yet, like you have."

He asked me, "Do you want children?"

I said, "I haven't really thought of that yet."

It was nice we had talked. Neither one of us really knew

the other. We had kind of been thrown together. We continued to talk for about an hour more.

It was morning and another day of investigating. *How will it go today? Will anybody be willing to talk to us?*

I had a lead on an elderly white woman in town. I was told she might know something about what happened to Nathaniel that night. I decided to go by myself and leave Agent Jones at the hotel to catch up on some paperwork. I didn't think bringing him long would be very helpful anyway.

As always, I told Agent Jones to be careful and not to let anyone he didn't know into the room. He got kind of mad. He said, "I'm no baby, I can handle myself."

I told him, "I know you can handle yourself, but I am afraid of what might happen to you if you are seen here alone."

He just shook his head back and forth.

I told him, "I'll pick up something for us to eat."

He said, "No more pimento, please!

My first visit was to the elderly white woman's house. Her name was Agnes Tooley. I had read in a report that she might have seen one of the men who killed Nathaniel.

I parked in front of her house. It looked like it hadn't been painted in about ten years as the paint was chipping off. She had a wooden fence that went all the way around the house.

I pushed the gate open and it squeaked very loudly. I think the whole neighborhood heard it. I walked up the flagstone path to the porch. I walked onto the wooden porch and it creaked as I made my way to the front door. There was an outside door with two screens. The inside door was open wide I knocked on the screen door several times.

Suddenly, I saw a figure coming toward the door. I could

barely make out the face the screen was thick and dark which made it hard to see what the person looked like.

I introduced myself. "Miss Tooley, My name is Agent Pierce. I'm from the Federal Bureau of Investigation. I would like to talk to you if I could." I showed her my badge.

She started speaking from behind the screen. "What the hell do you need to speak to me about?"

I told her, "I'm investigating a murder and I was told you might be able to help me. I would like to ask you a few questions if I could."

She said, "I don't know nothin' about no murder."

I became persistent. "I think maybe you do."

She suddenly became angry and said, "If you don't get off my property, I'm going to call the sheriff and have you removed."

Suddenly, I became angry. Since I had arrived I'd gotten nowhere with these ignorant people. I replied back, "Listen, Miss Tooley, either you can talk to me now or you can talk to me later. I rather we talked now, because if I leave now and have to come back, I'm not going to be in the best mood."

She seemed to back off. She opened the door and hurried me into her house.

She told me, "Sit in this chair." She sat across from me on the sofa and started talking. "My memory ain't what it used to be. I'm very old and tend to forget things."

I replied, "I hope your memory isn't as bad a you say it is. Whatever you tell me will be in the strictest confidence. No one other than myself will know about it."

She seemed hesitant to tell me anything. It seemed that even white people were unwilling to talk to us. I pressed Miss Tooley for any information she had. I saw in her face that she was frightened, afraid that if she talked, something might happen to her. It seemed to be the normal attitude, whether the person was white or black.

She began to open up a little as I asked her questions. She wouldn't answer some though.

She said, "I will only tell you why they killed that young boy. You want to know why they killed that little colored boy. I'll tell you why. Because he made a pass at a little white girl. That's why."

I wanted more information. I said, "There has to be more that. I need to know. You have to tell me."

She began to tell me the whole story. "Well, this is what I heard. You see that little colored boy was buying something from this store. So was this young little white girl. She was a pretty little girl with blonde hair. I think her name was Sarah Jean. He said something to her, probably something very vulgar. Her mother overheard it, grabbed her daughter and left the store It was soon all over town I heard a day or two later that they had found the boy and punished him."

I asked her, "Who punished him?"

She looked at me and said, "That's all I know."

I asked her, "What store?"

She told me, "Anderson's General Store. It's on Main and Clasdale."

I wrote everything down. I pressed her some more, but she refused to give any more information. She got up from the sofa and walked towards the front door. She said, "I think you better go now. I'm feeling somewhat tired."

I walked to the door. I thanked her and put out my and to shake hers. She simply stood there and looked at my hand. I opened the door and left.

As I walked to the car, all sorts of thoughts went through my head. *Finally, I might have a lead and the reason why he was murdered.*

I decided to drive back to the center of town. I wanted

to speak to the sheriff first. I wanted to know if he knew anything about it. If he did, he probably wouldn't tell me anyway, but I still wanted to talk to him. There seemed to be a cover-up going on, mostly because of fear and ignorance.

I walked into the sheriff's office. Deputy Hank was sitting at his desk doing a crossword puzzle. *This guy is totally useless as a human being.*

I told him, "I need to see Sheriff Crawford."

He said, "I have to see if he's in." He got up and walked over to the sheriff's door. He stopped and turned around and asked, with a smirk on his face, "Where's your little black buddy at?"

I just stared at him. I didn't want to waste any of my time on him.

He came out and said, "The sheriff is willing to see you, you can go in."

I walked in. The room smelled like an old cigar. He was sitting at his desk, chomping on what was left of a cigar.

He looked up and said, "Have a seat, Agent Pierce. It is Agent Pierce, isn't it?"

I replied back, "I'm surprised you remember my name."

He just smiled. I started asking, "About Nathaniel Johnson . . ."

He said, "Who the hell is Nathaniel Johnson?"

I said, "I think you know who Nathaniel Johnson is."

He said, "I don't think so. Could you refresh my memory?"

I told him, "Nathaniel was the young Negro boy that was found hung in a tree."

He said, "Oh, yeah, that little nigger boy. Yeah, I remember now. That's a damn shame what happened to him."

I asked him, "Did you bother investigating this crime?"

He replied back, "Yes, I did, but the funniest thing is

24

that no one saw or knows everything about it. I actually think the Ku Klux Klan had something to do with this."

I knew he was lying. He was probably involved in the crime himself. I said, "I don't believe you."

The smile that was usually on his face suddenly disappeared. He leaned forward in his chair across his desk and took the cigar out of his mouth.

He began to speak. "Are you calling me a liar, Agent Pierce? 'Cause if you are, I don't take too kindly when someone accuses me of lying."

I leaned forward in my chair until we were almost face to face. I said, "I find it hard to believe that someone like you, who probably knows everything and anything that goes on in this town can't even tell me a little about what happened that night when Nathaniel Johnson was murdered."

He leaned back into is chair and said, "You want to know, fine, I'll tell you. There were no eyewitnesses. Nobody saw nothing. I investigated this crime fully. I turned up nothing. Nobody has ever come forward with any information about it whatsoever. How can I arrest anybody if I don't know who did it?? Are you satisfied with that answer?"

He was right on that point. I asked him, "Can I have all your paperwork you have?"

At first he refused, so I told him, "I will get a search warrant and have a swarm of FBI agents down here in your office."

He decided to comply. He got up and walked to his door. He shouted for Deputy Hank. "Deputy, I want you to get all the paperwork we have on that Johnson death and give it to Agent Pierce."

The deputy replied, "Are you sure, Sheriff Crawford, you want me to do that?"

Sheriff Crawford screamed back, "I told you what to do,

now do it." He turned to me and said, "You're not going to find anything in there that I haven't told you about."

Deputy Hank handed me a small binder. I put it under my arm and walked out the door. I got into my car and opened it up to read. Sheriff Crawford was right. There wasn't a heck of a lot in the file. He had talked to a few people, but no one had seen anything.

I read the autopsy report. It wasn't pleasant. Apparently, before they hung Nathaniel, he was beaten severely. The two photos in the file were hard to look at. One was of Nathaniel Johnson hanging in the tree. I think he was already dead before they hung him. The other picture had been taken sometime the next day.

There wasn't much to go on. I thought, *We will never be able to solve this and bring to justice anyone for this crime. All the leads are leading us nowhere. Whomever we spoke with doesn't know anything, didn't see anything, or were unwilling to talk to us.*

I was becoming pessimistic as I drove back to the motel. It had not been as productive a day as I hoped it would be. *Hopefully, Agent Jones was able to get some things done in my absence.*

I walked to the door. I did my usual knocks, but no one answered. I knocked again even harder. Still no one answered the door. I didn't have a key. I had left it with Agent Jones in case he wanted to go out for a little bit. I started to worry.

I went down to the manager's office. I told him, "I locked myself out of my motel room. Do you have another key?"

He said, "I do." He gave me a key and said, "I want it back."

I ran back up to the door, opened and closed it quickly. I didn't see Agent Jones anywhere. I checked the bathroom, but still nothing I started to panic. *What if someone grabbed him?* I was afraid for his life.

I looked around. None of his things had been touched. His clothes were still there. There was no briefcase, nothing. I was about to call the Atlanta field office when all of sudden I heard someone at the door. I got up, took my gun out of the holster, and took the safety off. As the door started to open, I pointed my gun with my finger on the trigger. A face appeared. It was Agent Jones.

He looked at me with a surprised look. He said, "I hope you're not about to shoot me."

I put my gun down and said, "You nearly scared the shit out of me. Where the hell were you?"

He replied, "I was sick of being cooped up in this room. I decided to go and do some investigating of my own."

I wasn't very happy about it and I said, "You know you could have been seen by the motel manager. What if he called one of his redneck buddies? I might have come back and seen you hanging from a tree."

He said, "I told you I can take care of myself. You don't have to worry about me."

I said, "You know you could have messed up the investigation. Where would we be then?

He turned to me and said, "I'm sorry all right. Just get off my back about it."

I decided not to say any more. I wanted things to cool down. I needed to tell Agent Jones about the information that I had gotten. I said, "Jones, I might have gotten some leads. Also the sheriff gave me a file on Nathaniel Johnson's murder. It's pretty disturbing, but I think you should read it."

I handed him the file and he started going through it. He said, "There's not much in here, is there?"

I shook my head no. I turned and went into the bathroom. I needed to wash up a little. Suddenly, I heard Agent Jones say, "Oh, Christ!"

I walked back in the room. He was reading the autopsy

report and looking at the photo. He looked at me and said, "Did you see what they did to this little boy?"

I just looked at Agent Jones. I didn't know what to say. I had a feeling it would happen, but still he needed to see the photos. Hopefully, it wouldn't interfere with his judgment about our assignment. I hoped he could keep his feelings for what he saw deep down inside of him.

He handed me the file back and I put it in my briefcase.

I asked him, "What did you do today?"

He said, "I went back and talked to Mrs. Johnson, Nathaniel's grandmother. I thought maybe I could get some more information from her. I also talked to some of the people that live around them."

Agent Jones piqued my interest, so I asked him, "So what did you learn?"

He replied, "I think I might have a positive I.D. on the car."

Excited, I asked him, "Really, what kind of car was it?"

Agent Jones continued about the car. "Well, I think it might be either a '61 or '62 Belvedere station wagon. Also they think the color might have been either dark red or burgundy."

I thought, *Great, this could be the big break in the case we need.* I pressed Agent Jones for more on the car. "Did they get a license plate number?"

He replied, "No. It was too dark and it happened so fast."

I told Agent Jones, "This is great. I know we can probably find who owned this vehicle through the state's registration office for motor vehicles."

After all we'd been through the last few days, we had finally found a credible lead. Hopefully, it would pay off.

Two

I got on the phone and told the field office to get in touch with the vehicle registration office and see who here in Miner's Bluff owned such a car. Hopefully we would get an answer soon.

I told Agent Jones, "You done good."

He smiled back and said, "Now don't you feel bad for yelling at me earlier?"

I told him, "Yes, and don't do it again."

I was getting a little excited. Maybe after we got the information back from the registration office, things would fall into place.

I told Agent Jones, "I think we should go back out again and talk to people who we spoke with so far. If and when we find out who the person or people that murdered little Nathaniel Johnson were, I want these people I talked to so far to be witnesses for the prosecution, when and if it ever comes to trial.

First I went back to Miss Tooley.

She asked me, "What do you want this time?'

I told her, "I need to see you. We might have found who murdered Nathaniel Johnson. You might have to testify in court."

She said, "I was mistaken about what I said and that I will not testify in court."

I told her, "You could be subpoenaed."

"I don't know what you mean by that."

I told her.

She said, "I will lie if you do that."

Something must have happened because she changed her story.

Agent Jones went to Mrs. Johnson's house, Nathaniel's grandmother. He told her about the information we had on the car that took her grandson.

She started to recant her story. She said, "I might have been mistaken in what I saw."

He then talked to the others who had given him some information about what they saw. They started to recant their stories too. Someone had scared them.

Things seemed to be unraveling before our eyes. People who we thought would be good witnesses were now going back on their stories. I knew the sheriff and his cronies had gotten to them. Everything we had done so far seemed to be falling apart. If we were ever going to solve the murder and get a conviction, we needed people to testify in court. Our chances of it happening were getting thinner by the minute.

Anyone who we wanted to talk to had probably already been corrupted by these people. The fear of these people was so thick in the town, it could be cut with a knife. My patience was starting to wear thin.

Who are these people? How could they have such a hold on so many people? I thought. *What can happen next?*

Agent Jones and I headed back to the motel. We seemed to be back to square one.

Agent Jones and I were going over the paperwork that needed to be filed. We had been in the motel for six days. I was somewhat worried about staying so long. I thought it would be better if we rented a room a few miles out of the town. I felt our safety was in danger. I had a feeling that we were being followed. Maybe I was being a little paranoid, but I didn't trust the motel manager as far as I could spit either.

It was about ten o'clock at night and I was getting ready for bed. Agent Jones was already lying down on his bed. I got up and turned out the light in the bathroom. Suddenly, I heard gunshots and saw the pieces of glass from the window flying. I fell to the floor. Agent Jones rolled onto the floor between his bed and mine. I needed to get my gun, so I crawled over to my bed. My gun was on the night table. Agent Jones was trying to get his too. I grabbed it and then crawled over to the door on my hands and knees. Agent Jones followed me.

The shooting stopped. I got up and opened the door quickly, throwing it against the wall. I peered out behind the one side of the wall. I had my gun cocked and ready to shoot anybody out there. I looked around, but I didn't see anything. The car must have already spun off. It was too dark out to see anything. I walked back into the motel room.

I asked Agent Jones, "Are you all right?"

He checked himself out and nodded. "That was pretty damn close, if I say so myself," Agent Jones said.

I said, "This will be our last night in this motel room. Early tomorrow morning we will be checking out. I don't think they were meaning to kill us. They could have broken down the door and just shot us outright. I think they were trying to scare us."

Agent Jones gave me a funny look and said, "Well, it worked. This scares the living shit of out of me."

I told Agent Jones, "One of us is going to have to stay up to keep watch while the other sleeps. I will stay up first. We will sleep for three hours at a time. I'm afraid they might come back and finish the job. This way if they do, one of us will be prepared."

It was finally morning. I wanted to get out of the motel and town as quickly as possible. I walked to the manager' office to pay our bill. He was sitting behind the counter feeding his fat face.

He said, "What can I do for you, mister?"

I said, "I need my bill. I'm leaving today."

He went back to his desk and came back with a piece of paper. He said, "Let's see you stayed here six days at ten dollars a pop. That'll be sixty dollars, please."

I took out my wallet and paid him.

He said, "I need you to sign this, please. This will be your receipt." I signed the receipt.

I was about to leave when he said, "I heard there was a little commotion going on down at your room last night. I hope nothing's broken." He stood there with a smirk on his face.

I said, "Not much, just some bullet holes in your window. You better get them fixed before it rains."

I walked out the door and back to the room. Agent Jones was starting to load the car. I saw from a distance the car was listing to one side. I walked over to the right side of the car. *Great, two tires are flat.*

We had already used the spare, so I told Agent Jones, "Stop loading up the car. It isn't going to be going anywhere soon."

I went back into the room and called the Atlanta field office. I said, "We need another car. Bring down two spares for it too."

It would take about an hour and half for the car to arrive, so Agent Jones and I decided to take a walk. The countryside was really beautiful.

I wondered, *How can a place like this be so beautiful and so ugly at the same time?*

As we walked, Agent Jones told me about his childhood

in Georgia. "You know, Pierce, when I was little I used to live in a little town like this. We didn't have much, but it didn't matter. We had fun. I'd go down to this fishin' hole and fish there with my friends. We would never catch nothing, but we did it anyway. Life seemed slow and serene back then. Even with all the problems, I do have some good memories."

We must have walked about two miles when we came across a church. We heard the faint sound of singing. Agent Jones started to walk towards it, but I stayed back in the road.

I yelled, "Agent Jones, I think we should head back now."

He turned to me and said, "C'mon, it's the Sabbath anyway. What are you, an atheist?"

I told him, "No."

I began to walk towards the church with him. It was a small white church with reddish front doors. Agent Jones started up the steps.

I said, "What are you doing?" He turned to me and waved his hand for me to come up the steps, but I stayed down at the bottom. I said, "Let's go now, Jones."

He just smiled and slowly opened the door wide open and said, "C'mon, Pierce, after last night I think we need to thank God we're still alive."

I walked up the steps and both of us entered the church. As we did, it seemed like everyone turned around. There was absolute silence. One could hear a pin drop. There was some space in the back pew for us to sit down. I tried to maneuver over to the pew, trying not to look too obvious. It didn't work. We could hear the people mumbling under their breaths.

Agent Jones got up and said, "Sorry about this, please continue with your sermon, Reverend." I felt embarrassed and just kept my head down.

Suddenly, the reverend said, "My friends, it looks like we have some new members. Don't be embarrassed, everyone is welcome in God's house."

The organ started to play. The choir that was in the front of the church and off to the side, started to sing. I didn't really know what they were singing. It was a Baptist church and I was Lutheran. It sounded good though. I looked over at Agent Jones, who was clapping his hands and rocking back and forth. It seemed like everyone in the church was doing so, except me.

The singing stopped. The reverend got up from where he sat and started to speak to the congregation. "Everyone in here is a child of God. You are all made in His image whether you are black or white, red or yellow. He loves you all. He welcomes all and we welcome all."

The reverend continued with the service while agent Jones and I tried to blend in until it was over.

When the service was finally over, I told Agent Jones, "We better start heading back to the motel." I was afraid that the agents bringing the car would be waiting while we were still at the church and wondering where we were. They might think that something horrible happened to us.

Agent Jones wanted to speak with the reverend first. He said, "Wait till all the people leave, then I'll talk to him."

I gave him a look, but I guess it was okay. We waited until everyone had left the church. As the people walked past us, they looked unsure of what to make of us—a black and a white man both dressed in black suits.

After the last person left, Agent Jones walked to the front of the church where the reverend was cleaning up things before leaving. Agent Jones walked right up to him. I stayed a couple of feet away.

He put out his hand and said, "Reverend, sir, my name is Agent Jones. That man over there is my partner, Agent

Pierce. We're with the FBI, I'd like to ask you a few questions if I could."

I thought he was quite bold, but I couldn't fault him. We still needed help on the case and maybe the man could help us.

The reverend looked to be in his early 60s, his hair was mostly dark black, but graying on the side. He wore round-lensed glasses. He was short and stout. The reverend put out his hand to shake with Agent Jones.

He said, "My name is Otis Jackson. I'm glad to meet you, my son."

Agent Jones turned to me and waved his hand for me to come closer. I walked over to him and Reverend Jackson. I shook the reverend's hand.

He said, "What do you fine young men need to speak to me about?"

I decided to let Agent Jones handle it. He might be able to get more out of him.

Agent Jones said, "There was a young Negro boy killed about two months ago. My partner and I are investigating it. We just want to ask you some questions about it."

He looked at me and then at Agent Jones. He said, "Come back to my office. We can have some privacy there."

We both followed him. He opened the door to his office, which wasn't very big. There was barely enough room for two people.

He said, "Excuse the way it looks, I'm somewhat of a slob." I smiled at him. He continued talking, "Please sit down. May I get you something to drink? I think one of our matrons who helps me here has made some coffee earlier."

Both Agent Jones and I said, "No."

Agent Jones reiterated, "Like I said out there, my partner and I are investigating a murder of this young boy. His name was Nathaniel Johnson."

He took his glasses off, pulled a handkerchief out of his pocket and started to clean them. He said, "Yes, I knew Nathaniel Johnson." Finally he was saying something. He continued, "He always attended the church service regularly. He was fine young man. He was good at school, never a problem. I did his burial service." He became sad, almost to the point of weeping.

I decided to ask a question. "Reverend Jackson, do you know anything about what happened to him that night?"

He turned and looked at me and nodded his head. *This is wonderful, this might break open our case.*

I thought, *Maybe he saw the men or maybe he saw the car.* I didn't care. I just wanted to know what he knew. I pressed him for more information. Agent Jones had his pad out to write it all down.

The reverend began talking again. "I was driving back to my house down Willow Road. You see, I live about five miles from here near the outskirts of the town. I could see this commotion going on about maybe five hundred feet in front of my car. I decided to stop and pulled over. I stayed in my car and watched it. There were three men. I couldn't see their faces, it was dark. I didn't know what was going on. Suddenly, all three got back into the car and started to drive towards me. I became very frightened. As they passed, I looked straight ahead. I was afraid to look right at them."

He stopped suddenly. He took the handkerchief back out of his pocket and wiped both eyes. He then started talking again. "I wanted to look, but I just couldn't. I drove home as fast as I could. I ran into my house and locked the door. I hoped I wasn't followed. My wife heard me come in. I was shaking uncontrollably. She asked me what was wrong, but I couldn't speak." He paused again.

Agent Jones said, "Reverend Jackson, if you want to stop now, we'll understand."

I became angry at Agent Jones, so I turned to him with a look. He looked at me and held his hand up. He shook his hand back and forth as if to say no. I think he wanted me to wait few minutes until the reverend could compose himself again.

He said, "No, I'm all right. That's all I can tell you, I wish I could tell you more."

I decided to ask another question. "Sir, you didn't happen to notice what make or model or color the car was?"

The reverend, who had been looking down at his desk, looked up. He said, "It was a station wagon. I don't know the make or model. I'm not very good at knowing cars. It was either dark red or maroon. I couldn't really tell it was very dark and I was trying not to look."

Agent Jones got up and walked towards the door. He asked me, "Can we go outside for a few minutes?"

We got up and excused ourselves. We walked outside the office door.

Agent Jones whispered to me. "Pierce, I think he could help us more. He's giving a lot of good information. I think he probably knows more, but he's afraid. We need to get his address where he lives and maybe talk to him more at his home." I thought it was a good idea.

We walked back in.

Agent Jones spoke to the reverend. "Sir, you've been very helpful. We'd like to get your address, just in case we need to speak to you some more."

He pulled out a piece of paper, wrote his address on it, and handed it to Agent Jones. Agent Jones put out his hand to shake the reverend's and said, "Thank you, sir, for your time. You don't know how helpful you've been. We're sorry if we have been a bother to you."

He smiled and put out his hand to shake both our

hands. He said, "You been no bother. You're just doing your job."

He got up from his desk and walked us to the front door of the church. We started walking back to the motel.

I told Agent Jones, "We need to get back as quickly as possible."

While we walked, we discussed all the information we had gotten during the day.

Agent Jones turned to me and said, "He knows more, I just know it."

I asked, "What do you mean?"

He said, "I can tell, that's all."

We finally made it back to the motel. My feet were killing me. I was hot and tired. I saw a couple of men sitting on our car. We walked towards them.

One of them shouted, "Where the hell were you guys? We've been here for a half-hour. We were going to get a shit load of agents down here looking for you."

Both Agent Jones and I laughed.

One of the agents put his hand out to shake mine and said, "My name is Agent Hollis. That one over there is Agent Thorn and that's Calder." They waved at us and said hello.

Agent Hollis said, "Put out your hand." I put my hand you and he dropped a set of keys in it. He said, "See that car over there? That's your new car. Don't do anything to this one, because you're not getting another one."

He laughed and walked away. One of the agents hopped into our old car and started to drive away. He laid down on the horn as he did. The other two agents got into the other car and sped off. They kicked up some gravel that hit us in the face.

We need to find a nice place to stay, but where? I thought it would be better if we looked for some place out of town, way out of town. It was too dangerous to stay out in the open.

Three

We packed the car and headed on our way out of town. We drove for a while down a long dirt road.

Agent Jones turned to me and said, "I'm kind of hungry, maybe we can stop and get something to eat."

Agent Jones was always thinking with his stomach. I drove a little farther when I saw along the roadside what looked like a place to eat.

I pulled over and parked near it. There weren't very many cars parked in front. I wondered if it was open.

As we walked in, everyone turned around. All I saw were black faces. Apparently we were in the black section of town. I guessed the town's black people congregated there.

Agent Jones turned to me and said, "If you want to leave, I'll understand."

I said, "That's all right, as least in here no one is going to try to kill us, I hope."

He laughed and we both walked towards the counter.

A young, pretty black woman behind the counter asked, "Can I help you gentlemen?"

Agent Jones answered, "Yes, we would like a table so we can order some food."

She walked from behind the counter and said, "My name is Joline. I'll be your hostess. You two, follow me."

Jones and I both obliged. She walked to a table that was against the wall. We sat down.

She turned to me and said, "We don't get many people like you in here."

I thought she was being sarcastic. I retorted back, "You mean, not many white people."

She broke out in a laugh. She said, "No, not that, we don't get too many people walking in here dressed the way you two are. Look around, nobody in here is dressed in a suit. Once they leave church, off goes the good clothes. Can I get you gentlemen something to drink? Maybe a beer?"

Agent Jones said, "Yes."

I told here, "I just want coffee."

She said, "C'mon, honey, you're going to drink coffee when it's about a hundred and four degrees today?"

I said, "Okay, I'll have a beer."

She said, "Now that's more like it. Relax, ain't nobody in here going to bother you."

Agent Jones leaned over to me and said, "Pierce, loosen up for Christ sake. These people don't care who or what you are."

I was a little uptight. I had never been the only white person anywhere before and felt a little uncomfortable. I thought *Maybe this is how a lot of these people feel when they are around whites.*

Our hostess came back with the beers. She said, "Here are your beers. I just want to let you know that our house special is deep fried catfish. This comes with a choice of collard greens, beans and rice or grits as two of your side orders. Oh, you also get our homemade biscuits."

Agent Jones said, "We'll both have the house special with a side order of collard greens and grits." Before I could speak, our hostess was already gone.

I asked Agent Jones, "Why the hell did you order for me? I wanted to see a menu so I could see what they had."

Agent Jones retorted, "Even if she gave you a menu, you wouldn't have known half of what was on it anyway."

I thought, *I don't know, but you seem to be getting a little pushy.*

We began talking about the case. We seemed to have a near positive I.D. on the color of the car. All we had to do was wait for the information from the state vehicle registration department. We could narrow the car down to someone who lived in town, but it wouldn't be enough We needed someone to identify the people who took Nathaniel Johnson that night. Someone in town had to have seen someone or something.

Joline came towards us carrying a tray above her head. She stood next to me and put a plate in front of me, then she put the other in front of Agent Jones. She said, "There you go, boys, eat up." She then put a bottle of ketchup on the table. "I think you're going to need that," she said as she walked away.

I looked down at my plate. There was a huge piece of breaded fish sitting on it that took about half the plate up. Beside it was something that looked like spinach and something that looked like thick cream of wheat. I hadn't even cut a piece of fish off before Agent Jones was halfway finished with his meal.

He looked at me and said, "Don't worry, it's not going to bite you. It's good, try it."

I took a small piece of fish and ate it. It wasn't bad. A little greasy, otherwise it tasted good. I tried the collard greens. I started to chew it, but after a few seconds I wanted to spit it out. I took a big gulp of beer to swallow it and wash the taste out of my mouth.

Agent Jones started to laugh. He said, "It's kind of bitter, isn't it?"

I said, "It sure is."

He took the saltshaker and started to shake some on the

41

collard green and grits. He then took a big chunk of butter and put it on top. He said, "Now, try it, it should taste a little better."

I tried to eat it again, but it still was too bitter for me.

He then said, "I guess it's an acquired taste."

I continued eating the fish. It wasn't bad and I was sort of hungry. When I looked over at Agent Jones, he had finished everything on his plate. I just shook my head.

Suddenly, he let out a big burp and then excused himself. He said, "That was sure some good eatin'."

I told him, "Next time let me do the ordering."

I called for our hostess. I said, "Excuse me, miss, my partner and I would like the check now."

She said, "Don't you want any dessert? We got some great pies. Our specialty is pecan pie."

Agent Jones said, "No, we're both full. We couldn't eat another bite."

She said, "No bother, sweetie, I'll be right over with it."

While we talked, I saw Reverend Jackson came in the restaurant. He walked over to the counter and waited. I got up and walked over to him.

I said, "Fancy meeting you here, Reverend Jackson."

He looked at me with a surprised look and said, "Oh, it's you, Agent Pierce. I would have never expected to see you here."

I said, "Oh, Agent Jones dragged me in here. He was really hungry."

He just laughed. He continued talking to me, "I would like to invite you over tonight to my house for dinner if you don't mind."

I said, "Not at all. I know Agent Jones would be happy to."

He said, "Come around six. You already have directions to my house."

Joline came out with a box in her hand and put it down in front of Reverend Jackson. She said, "That will be a dollar and a quarter, Reverend Jackson."

He handed her the money and was about to leave. He said, "I hope you like pecan pie, because that was for dessert."

I went back to the table. Joline came over with the check and placed it face down on the table. I went to pick it up, but Agent Jones got to it first.

He said, "Don't worry, this one is on me." We got up and made our way to leave.

Joline yelled at us as we were leaving, "Come back again, you two honeys are always welcome."

We got in the car and made our way out of the town. We needed to find a place to stay where hopefully we could go unnoticed. We drove for a while, but didn't see any place to stay. Finally, we came to a small hotel. I pulled into the parking lot.

I told Agent Jones, "Stay in the car."

As always, he didn't listen. He walked with me into the hotel's registration office. A young girl was behind the counter.

Agent Jones stayed near the front door. I asked, "Do you have a room?" She kept peering over my shoulder to look at Agent Jones. I told her, "The room is for me and my friend.

She looked at me and then at Jones. She said, "I'm sorry, sir, we don't rent rooms to no Negroes."

I told her, "You're not renting a room to a Negro, you're renting it to me.

She insisted, "I can't rent the room to you."

I asked her, "Why?"

She said, "Mister, I'm just doing my job. If I rented a room to you, I would lose my job." She continued, "Mister, I don't want no trouble. If I have to, I'll call the cops."

I was about to tell her that we were with the FBI, but

thought we'd had enough trouble already. Anyway, she really didn't need to know who we were. I told her, "I am going to be coming back and you are going to be in big trouble."

I drove to a small store and picked up a local paper. I thought, *Maybe we can find a room to rent at someone's house.*

I started looking in the paper. There were rooms to rent, but every one of them said: "Whites Only." I thought we'd have to drive all the way to Atlanta to find a place to stay. I was really getting frustrated with the madness of it all. It was getting late. We needed to find a room or we would have to sleep in the car.

It was almost 5:30. We had to be at the reverend's house by 6:00. I found the nearest gas station and pulled into it. I needed some gas and to use the bathroom.

I told Agent Jones, "Wait by the bathroom while I distract the gas station owner." I knew Agent Jones needed to use the bathroom too, but they probably wouldn't let him.

I walked into the office. I told the owner, "I need five dollars worth of gas and I want to use the bathroom."

He turned around and grabbed a key from the back wall. He said, "It's around the side."

I walked around to the side. Agent Jones was waiting patiently there.

He said, "Come on, I really have to go."

I put the key int he door. I turned it, but it wouldn't open. I kept twisting the key and then I banged against the door. The door seemed to be stuck. I told Agent Jones, "Maybe if we both lean against it at the same time it will open."

I turned the key and, on the count of three, we both leaned hard against the door. Suddenly, it sprung open.

The bathroom was dark, dingy, and dirty. It looked like it hadn't been cleaned in ages. I didn't really care though. We both needed to go to the bathroom. Unfortunately, there was only one toilet to use and, of course, it didn't have a door. Agent Jones went first, then me.

I told him, "I think we need to wash up a little before going to see the reverend."

I turned on the water and, of course, only cold water came out, even out of the one marked "hot." There was an old-looking bar of soap in the soap dish. It looked greasy, but I used it anyway. We cleaned ourselves up as well as we could.

I told Agent Jones, "Wait in the bathroom until I come for you. I don't want the station manager to see you and start any trouble."

I went back out and over to the car. The manager was still filling the car. He said, "That will be three dollars, mister." I gave him a ten.

He said, "You're going to have to come back to the office with me. I don't carry that much change."

He handed me my change and said, "That's a nice car you got there, mister. You some kind of businessman?"

I said, "Yes, I am. I sell real estate."

He said, "That's nice. You know there are a lot of places you can buy down here. The only problem is that you're going to have live with niggers."

I said, "I don't think I have a problem with that."

Suddenly, the smile came off his face. He said, "I think you better leave now, mister."

I thought I'd worn out my welcome, so I drove around to the side and honked the horn. Agent Jones came out of the bathroom. I backed out, turned the car around, and headed for the highway. As I did so, the man from the gas station ran out of his office and stared at me as I drove by. I decided to wave to him.

I told Agent Jones, "Wave at him, too." I thought, *I better floor it. Who knows who he's going to tell?*

45

We drove for a while, headed for Reverend Jackson's house. I asked Agent Jones, "Read me the directions."

I listened to him and did what he told me. Suddenly we found the road we needed to go down—Peachtree Road. We needed to make a left. It was the last house down the road.

I drove slowly looking for a bluish-green color house. I saw it on my right side. It was quite nice looking. It was two floors instead on the usual one and had a wooden porch that went halfway around it. A large swinging chair hung from the ceiling of the porch. We got out and walked towards the house. We went up the steps to the front door.

I knocked and an elderly woman appeared at the door. She opened the outside door and said, "Won't you come in. You must be the two gentlemen that my husband has been talking about." She was smiling the whole time he spoke. "My name is Loretta, I'm happy to meet you both."

She put out her hand to shake ours. I introduced myself and Agent Jones.

She said, "Please follow me." She walked us over to a sofa in the living room. "Both of you please sit down, while I go and get my husband."

I looked around. It was quite beautiful inside, unlike the other black people's houses we had been in before. Reverend Jackson seemed to be doing very well for himself.

A few minutes later, Reverend Jackson came into the living room. I was about to get up to shake his hand when he said, "No, no, don't get up. Just sit there and relax. Dinner won't be ready for another fifteen minutes."

He went over to the mantle over the fireplace. He picked up a small pouch and what appeared to be a pipe. He began to fill the pipe, pushing in as much tobacco as he could. He then struck a match against the fireplace and lit the pipe. The aroma smelled good.

He said, "You gentlemen don't mind if I smoke my pipe, do you?"

I said, "Not at all, Reverend, this is your house anyway."

He laughed. He walked back over to us and sat in a chair across from Agent Jones and myself.

"You boys didn't have a hard time finding this place, did you?" he asked.

I said, "It was no problem at all."

There was lull in the conversation, then Agent Jones asked him. "Reverend Jackson, how long have you lived here in Miner's Bluff?"

He replied, "All my life."

Agent Jones then asked, "How long have you been reverend at the church?"

"Oh, it must be going on about forty years, I think. Ever since the twenties."

Mrs. Jackson came into the living room and said, "Well, I hate to disturb you fine gentlemen, but dinner is ready."

Everyone got up and followed Mrs. Jackson into the dining room. She turned to me and said, "Mr. Pierce, you can sit here, Mr. Jones you can sit across from Mr. Pierce. My husband always has to sit at the head of the table."

We both sat the table. Reverend Jackson was already seated.

Mrs. Jackson said, "I hope you young men are hungry. I made my special—porkchops in red gravy and rice. Some mashed potatoes and green beans and, of course, for dessert pecan pie."

I was just glad it wasn't collard greens and grits. I thought I'd had enough of them already for a day.

She started to bring the food in and set it down in front of us. I felt bad sitting there doing nothing. I asked her, "Can I help?"

She said, "Absolutely not, you're our guests. What kind of hostess would I be if I made my guests work?"

She smiled and I sat back down. *She's such a sweet woman,* I thought.

Everything smelled good. Mrs. Jackson came out of the kitchen and sat at the far end of the table.

Reverend Jackson turned to me and said, "We always say a prayer before eating our meals."

I didn't have a problem with it. He put both his arms on the table and held out his hand, as did Mrs. Jackson. Agent Jones grabbed his left hand right away. He looked at me and nodded towards Reverend Jackson's hand. I grabbed it and then I grabbed Mrs. Jackson's hand.

Reverend Jackson said, "Let us pray." He then closed his eyes and bowed his head down. I did the same. He began his prayer. "Thank you, Lord, for the meal that you have provided us with here today. We are so grateful for you blessings. Also, Lord, watch over the ones who cannot help themselves and bless these fine young men who sit before you. They're here on a great mission and need your guidance. Always your humble servant. Amen."

We began to eat. I have to say that the food was really good. I turned to Mrs. Jackson and said, "Mrs. Jackson, everything here is delicious. You're a wonderful cook."

She smiled and said, "Thank you, Mr. Pierce. I appreciate your compliment."

I said, "Please call me 'Daniel.' There is no need to be formal."

She said, "All right, Daniel. You can call me 'Loretta' then."

I said, "I'd rather not, you're so like my mother, I would find it disrespectful."

Reverend Jackson hadn't said a word. I think he was too busy eating his dinner. We were happy about having a nice dinner, but we were there for another reason—to see if Reverend Jackson knew more than he had told us earlier in the day. I thought he did, which was why he invited us to dinner. I hoped he would tell us more.

Finished with our dinner, Mrs. Jackson turned to me and said, "I hope all of you men have enough room for dessert. We're having Otis's favorite, pecan pie."

Agent Jones replied, "Well, Mrs. Jackson, if we don't, we'll make room."

Mrs. Jackson laughed a little, then got up and headed for the kitchen. She came back in with a large tray with slices of pie on it. She handed each one of us a piece and then excused herself. She said, "I'm going to have to leave you men now. There are dishes to be done."

We finished our pie. Reverend Jackson asked us to come into the office he had in the house. We followed him to a small office that was off the side of the living room.

He said, "Agent Jones, please shut the door."

He began to talk. "I didn't tell you everything I know when I spoke to you earlier today."

I hoped he was going to tell us that he had actually seen one of the persons who committed the murder.

Agent Jones looked at me and I looked at him. "What didn't you tell us earlier, Reverend Jones?"

Reverend replied, "Well, like I told you before, I didn't see the faces of the men in the car. It went by pretty fast. I did look in the rearview mirror as it was going down the road. I caught a glance of the license plate."

I was about to burst with excitement. *I can't believe it. This could break the case wide open.* I said to him, "What did you see?" We really needed to know. It would help us immensely if he could remember what he saw.

He said, "I think I remember almost all of the license plate numbers."

I got my notepad and pen. I asked him again, "Slowly tell me the license plate numbers."

He replied, "I think it was CVL-1575. I'm not totally sure."

I thought, *Even if we only have a few numbers, we can still match them with the report we'll be getting back from the vehicle registration office. Finally after so many dead ends, we might have something.* Even though it wasn't very much, it was still something. Once we identified the car, we would know who owned it. It could be the murderer.

I asked him, "Can you tell us any more?"

He said, "I'm sorry, that's all I know."

He had a scared look on his face. I truly believed he didn't know any more. I didn't press him about it.

Suddenly, there was a knock on the door. It was Mrs. Jackson. She peeked her head in the door and said, "I'm sorry to disturb you men but I've made a fresh pot of coffee and I thought maybe you might want some."

Both Agent Jones and I said, "No, thank you."

Reverend Jackson simply said, "Later Loretta." She smiled and closed the door.

It was time for us to leave. I turned to Agent Jones and said, "I think it's time for us to go. I think we bothered the reverend and his wife enough tonight. I don't want to stay or we're going to have to sleep in the car."

Reverend Jackson said, "Wait a minute." He left his office.

I thought, *Maybe he found either a motel or a place we can rent.*

He came back into his office and said, "Gentlemen, I've spoken to my wife about you staying here. I hate to tell you this, but there ain't no place that's going to rent a motel or room to you, as long as Agent Jones is with you. No offense, Agent Jones."

"None taken," Agent Jones responded.

We walked back out into the living room as Mrs. Jackson came from out of the kitchen.

I said to her, "I appreciate you letting us stay here. I hope we're not putting you out any."

She said, "Not at all. It will be nice to have some young people in our house. You see, both our sons are grown. My oldest's name is Marcus and he lives in Michigan with his family; my other son is Cletis and he lives in Illinois. He's not married and has no family."

I thought it was nice of them because they didn't really know us. I guess they trusted us more than someone else. We all sat down on the couch. Mrs. Jackson brought in some coffee to drink. She sat on the arm of the chair that her husband sat at.

She asked, "What are you men talking about?"

Reverend replied, "Oh, just things, dear."

I knew she knew who we were, but she didn't know why we were there. I decided to take a chance. I thought she might tell us something, yet I was afraid that Reverend Jackson might become angry and throw us both out of the house. I said, "Oh, Mrs. Jackson, I don't know if your husband told you about us. If he didn't you might not want us here."

She got a strange look on her face. She said, "My husband told me you're from the government. What was it? Oh, yes, the FBI."

I replied, "Your husband was correct. That doesn't bother you?"

She said, "Should it?"

I said, "No, but since we've been here, we haven't gotten the warmest welcome. Also we could be putting you in danger."

She said, "Let me tell you. It couldn't be any more dangerous with you here than it has been in the past. We been threatened with murder. We had our animals killed. We had

51

rocks thrown through our windows. It can't get any more dangerous than that."

I said, "I see your point."

I asked her, "Did your husband tell you why we are here?"

She said in a low whisper, "Yes." She continued. "It was horrible what they did to that little boy. He didn't harm nobody. Did my husband tell you he was the one that cut him down from that tree?"

Suddenly, Reverend Jackson turned quickly to his wife and said in a very stern voice, "Hush, Loretta."

She retorted, "No, Otis, I won't be silent about this."

I fell back into my chair. I turned to Reverend Jackson and said, "I didn't know that. It must have been a horrible thing for you to see. I can't imagine how you felt right then."

He replied, "He deserved better. I blame myself." He put his head in his hand and started to weep.

His wife laid her head against his and rubbed his left shoulder, and said over and over, "It's all right, my baby. It's all right."

I felt bad. I felt like I'd caused it. I decided not to ask any more questions about it. It still affected him deeply and I thought it best to leave it alone for the time being. It was getting late and Agent Jones and I needed to be up early and continue our investigation.

I got up and said, "I think I'd like to go to bed now."

Agent Jones said to me, "I just want to finish my coffee, I'll be right there."

Mrs. Jackson got up off the arm of the chair and said, "Follow me."

We went upstairs.

She said, "I have the beds all made up already." She walked down the hall a little and stopped. She opened the door on my left and said, "This is where you and Franklin can sleep. There's two nice beds in there. Hardly been slept on." She pointed towards another door down the hall and said, "That's the bathroom and over there is our room."

I said, "I hope I won't get them mixed up."

She smiled and said, "I hope you enjoy your stay." She turned around and headed back downstairs.

I walked in. It was a nice room. It had two nice-sized beds and a large dresser. There was a sink and over it was a mirror. I walked back downstairs to get our suitcases out of the car. Mrs. Jackson was busy cleaning up.

I asked her, "Where's Agent Jones at?"

She said, "Oh, Franklin, he's in my husband's office talking to him."

I said, "Thanks."

I walked out to the car to get the suitcase.

While I did so, I thought, *What's Agent Jones doing? I don't like this at all. We are partners in this. There should be no secrets between us. Yet he insists on going out on his own, going behind my back. What is the big secret? If this is going to work, he's going to have to stop this.*

I walked back into the house with the suitcase and went up the stairs. I walked into the room. Agent Jones was on one of the beds bouncing up and down.

He said, "I got dibs on this one."

I didn't answer him. I put the suitcase against one of the side walls. I started to undress. As I did so, I started to ask Agent Jones some questions.

"What were you talking about with the reverend?" I asked.

He said, "What are you talking about?"

I replied, "When I came down, you weren't in the living room anymore. I asked Mrs. Jackson where you were at and she told me you were back in is office talking."

He said, "Yeah, what about it?"

I said, "Well, what were you talking about?" He didn't say anything. I thought he was ignoring me, so I asked him again, "What were you talking about?"

He turned to me with an angry look and said, "Just things, is that all right with you? It had nothing to do with the case. I just wanted to talk to someone."

I asked, "Why can't you talk to me? We're partners, aren't we? We can't have secrets between us. If he tells you something important I need to know it."

He replied, "I told you before it has nothing to do with the case."

Suddenly, he got up and walked over to me. When we were face to face, he said, "All right, you want to know what we talked about. I'll tell you what we talked about." He was sort of frightening me as he continued his tirade, "I'll tell what we talked about—what it's like to be a Negro in this country, especially down here in the south. The same thing year after year, being beaten and murdered just because of the color of your skin."

He stopped for a few seconds and walked over to the dresser and threw his watch on it. He said, "Do you think you can relate to that? I don't think so. Being white and all."

I said, "I told you if you need to talk, you can talk to me. I don't care who or what you are. It doesn't matter to me."

He replied, "Well, it matters to me. You don't understand. Sometimes I need to talk to someone, someone like Reverend Jackson."

I said, "I'm telling you, if you need to talk to me about anything, I mean anything, you can. We're partners."

He replied, "Yeah, we're partners, but that's all we're going to be. Once this is over you go back to living your nice beautiful life in New York and my people are still going to be living this rotten life down here. I don't want to talk about it anymore. I'm going to sleep."

He got in bed, pulled the cover up around him, and faced the wall.

I laid back in my bed and thought, *Is this the right thing for the field office to do? To send a black man down here to the south, especially one who had a lot of issues to deal with? What might happen if he is confronted? What will he do?* I started to worry a little as I fell asleep.

I looked at the clock. It was six o'clock in the morning. It was first good night's sleep we'd both had since coming to Miner's Bluff. We'd been on edge ever since, especially after the shootout at the motel.

I looked over at Agent Jones, who was sound asleep and snoring loudly. I walked over with a pillow in hand and hit him pretty hard. Suddenly, he sprang up out of bed and started to look around. I fell back into my bed laughing.

He said very angrily to me, "Very funny. You know you could have killed me."

I decided to take a shower. I walked down the hallway to the bathroom. The door was open. I thought, *Great, no one is in there.*

I tried to be as quiet as possible as I didn't want to disturb Reverend Jackson or his wife. I needed to make it as quick as possible. We had a lot to do.

After my shower, I peeked out into the hall. I didn't see anyone, so I made a mad dash to our bedroom. I only had a towel draped around me.

Agent Jones said, "Great, you're all done with your shower. I'll take mine now. I hope you left some hot water." He stopped before he went out the door. He turned around and said, "I'm sorry about last night. I hope you weren't offended. Sometimes I get a little cranky. It had nothing to do with you."

I said, "It's no problem, already forgotten." He turned and walked out the door.

After I dressed I decided to go downstairs and wait outside on the porch for Agent Jones. I was making my way to the front door when I heard a voice behind me. It was Mrs. Jackson.

She said, "Going already? Don't you want some breakfast? I made some scrambled eggs and bacon and some fresh corn muffins."

I didn't want to insult her and I was a little hungry, so I said, "Sure."

She went back into the kitchen and brought a plate in. There was so much food on it that I told her, "This is too much. I'm not going to be able to eat all of this."

She said, "Nonsense, you're a young man, you're not all grown up yet. Anyway, you need a good breakfast in the morning to get you going."

I thought after breakfast that Agent Jones and I would go back to Atlanta to our field office and see if they had gotten anything back on the car. I told Agent Jones.

He said, "That's fine, I think both of us need to get out of this town for a while."

I told Mrs. Jackson, "We will be out all day and probably won't be back at all today, but we might be back tomorrow. We are going back to Atlanta."

She said, "I hope you both are coming back. It's so nice having someone other than my husband in the house."

Agent Jones finished with breakfast and we were ready to go. We were about to walk out the door when Mrs. Jackson met us with a large paper bag in her hands.

She said, "Just in case you boys get hungry, I packed a few ham sandwiches and some slices of pie."

I took the bag from her and said, "We appreciate all you

have done." For some reason I then gave her a peck on the cheek.

Her eyes went open wide with surprise. She grabbed the side of her face and said, "Oh, my!"

Agent Jones looked at me and shook his head. As we walked down to the car, Agent Jones said to me, "You better stop that. You might end up going to sleep one night and waking up black." He let out a big laugh.

I said, "What's wrong with what I did?" He just continued laughing.

We were back in Atlanta and it was nice being back in a large city where I didn't feel out of place. I headed straight for the FBI field office. When I walked in there was a lot going on and people were rushing around. Our commander wanted to know how much information we had been able to obtain. I didn't think he would be very happy because we didn't have much.

I walked into his office. "Good morning, Commander Holden," I said.

He looked up from his desk. "Good morning to you, Agent Pierce," he replied. "How's the case going so far?"

I said, "Well, Commander, it started pretty dismal, but we seem to be making some progress."

He asked, "Have you caught the person or persons that did the killing yet?"

I said, "No, not yet, but we do have many credible leads and I think pretty soon, we'll have our people."

He said, "I hope so, we need to get this wrapped up as soon as possible. Headquarters is really on my case about getting this over with. Well, that's all for now, Agent Pierce."

I got up from my chair and said, "Thank you for your time, sir."

He smiled and I was on my way out of the office.

Four

I started looking for Agent Jones. He was over in the information bureau to see if the car license plate number that Reverend Jackson gave us matched a car in Miner's Bluff. I walked over to him.

He turned to me and said, "They're working on it now, Pierce. Hopefully it matches a car in town. The person who's getting the information told us it would be another day."

Agent Jones decided to leave early to visit his family who lived in Atlanta. I decided to go to my desk and check all the information that we already had on the case.

I would not see Agent Jones until the next day. The field office had apartments to live in while we were there working on the case. I decided to stay for the night since I had to wait for the information about the car. I decided to leave and get a good night's sleep and come in the next day

I was in the field office at the crack of dawn. Agent Jones was nowhere to be found. I had been at work for about an hour when as I was going through a file, Sandra, our information clerk, ran in.

She said, "I think I have a match for you."

I jumped from my chair. "Great! What do you have?"

She replied, "Well, there's a car that fits the description that you have us in Miner's Bluff. It's owned by someone named Pernel Williams. He lives at 1222 Sycamore Lane."

I thought, *This is the big break we need. Now we have a positive I.D. on the car.*

I was so happy that I grabbed Sandra and gave her a big kiss. She seemed startled when I did. I went looking for Agent Jones. We needed to get back to Miner's Bluff as quickly as possible. I found him conversing with a fellow agent.

I said, "Jones, you're not going to believe this. We have a positive ID on the car. The guy's name is Pernel Williams. I have his address and everything. We need to go back to Miner's Bluff."

He replied, "That's great, Pierce. Now comes the hard part."

I was surprised by his reaction. "What do you mean?"

He said, "What do you think, that we're just going to go down there and arrest him because he owns this car?"

I said, "It's a start."

He replied, "I'm telling you right now, if you think it was bad before, it's going to get a lot worse. These people don't care about the law. We need more than just him owning this car even to arrest him."

"I thought we would take a visit over to Pernel Williams's house to have a little talk with him."

We were back on our way to Miner's Bluff. I thought we had a lot going for us. We had a name and make of the car and the person who possibly owned it. Agent Jones wasn't so sure. Before leaving Atlanta, I went before a judge to get a search-and-seize order. If the car was there, I wanted to be able to confiscate it before Pernel Williams did anything with it.

I decided to bring Agent Jones with me when I went to see Pernel Williams. I was going to leave him back at the Jackson house, but I decided otherwise. I feared for his safety. We were going into hostile territory. As always, Agent

Jones fought me about it. He said he wasn't worried, but I sure was.

We needed to find Sycamore Lane. Even though the town wasn't big, one could easily get lost in it. There were some roads with many twists and turns, and many roads that didn't have signs. The dirt roads didn't have any lights either, so if traveling at night, one had a hard time finding their way around.

I found the road and drove down it. The address was 1222. It was difficult because there weren't many mailboxes with numbers on them. I must have driven a mile when finally I came upon it. It didn't look like much. It had a huge willow tree in the front yard that nearly covered the front of the house. It looked as if a good wind could blow it over. There was a fence around it, but no gate, and a driveway on the side, but no car.

I thought, *I wonder where it is?*

Agent Jones and I got out of the car. I looked around, as did Agent Jones. We didn't know what to expect. Someone could shoot from a window and we would never know it. To say I felt uncomfortable at the time was an understatement.

I walked slowly towards the house, always looking around. I felt eyes peering at us.

I walked onto the porch, which was quite rickety. I thought my foot would fall through it. I approached the door very quietly and knocked, keeping one hand on my gun. I wasn't taking any chances. Agent Jones was a few feet away from me surveying the area for anything unusual. No one answered, so I knocked harder.

Finally someone came to the door, an older-looking gentleman, probably in his late forties. His hair was graying and looked unkempt. He wore a dirty white t-shirt and looked like he hadn't shaved in days.

I said very forcefully, "Are you Pernel Williams?"

He said, "Who the hell wants to know?"

I said, "My name is Agent Pierce. I'm with the FBI. I need to speak to you."

He said, "What about?"

I said, "Sir, we can do this the easy way or the hard way. Either you're going to let me in and talk to me or I'm going to have to force my way in. Either way I don't care."

He said, "All right."

I told Agent Jones, "Come with me."

Mr. Williams' view was obstructed, so he really couldn't see Agent Jones, plus Agent Jones had his back turned to him. As soon as he turned around, Mr. Williams became upset.

He said, "I don't want that nigger near my house."

I said, "I'm sorry to hear that, Mr. Williams, but Mr. Jones is my partner and where I go, he goes."

He reluctantly decided to let us both in his house. The house was a pigsty. There was junk everywhere. It didn't smell very good. It smelled like old beer and garbage. Mr. Williams didn't smell very good either. He reeked of booze.

I told him, "Sit down. I need to ask you a few questions."

As I began the interrogation, Agent Jones started to look around the house.

Mr. Williams objected highly. "What the hell is he doing? He better not be stealing nothing of mine."

I reached into my suit coat pocket and pulled out the search warrant. I placed it on the coffee table in front of me. I said to Mr. Williams, "That's a search warrant. Look at it if you want. It allows me and my partner to look anywhere and to take anything. Do you understand me?"

He nodded his head. I was ready to start questioning him. I pulled out a picture similar to his car. I placed it in front of him. I asked, "Can I have your car registration?"

He pulled it out of his wallet. I checked the numbers. It

matched the one the reverend gave us and the one I had from the Department of Transportation. I said, "Is this car in the picture the same as the car you own?"

He picked up the picture and placed it back down. He simply said, "No."

I didn't believe him. I continued my interrogation. "I don't believe you. This car was seen at a crime. It was burgundy in color, same make as yours, with the same license plate numbers. Are you denying it's yours?"

He replied, "I'm telling you it's not mine. I don't own a car."

I continued, "I believe this car is yours. Your name is Pernel Williams, you live at 1222 Sycamore Lane, in the town of Miner's Bluff. The registration for the car has the same information and you're telling me it's not yours."

He said, "No, it's not the same. My car was stolen."

I said, "Your car was stolen. Did you file a report about it being stolen?"

He said, "No, I didn't."

I asked him, "Why not?" He just looked at me. I asked him again, "Why not?"

He replied, "'Cause I just didn't feel like it."

I said, "Someone steals your new car and you don't report it because you didn't feel like it. I don't believe you."

He said, "I don't give a rat's ass what you believe."

I thought, *Great, he's going to play this game.*

I decided to press harder. I told him about the murder of the young boy. "Someone saw you and two others. They can describe the car and you at the scene. You are going to be charged with the murder yourself if you don't talk."

He sat there stone-faced with no expression whatsoever. Then he started to speak. "You can have all the eyewitnesses you want. You have no way of proving it. Do you think that some police or court in this town is going to believe some outsider like you? You best just forget all of this and go back the way you came from and take your nigger friend with you," he said very coldly.

I said, "Fine, I hope you don't mind me looking around your house now do you? And don't try to stop me or I'm going to have about thirty FBI agents swarming your house."

While I was in the house looking for anything that might help us, Agent Jones looked around outside. I hadn't seen him since I started talking to Mr. Williams.

I told Mr. Williams, "I am keeping your car registration. It might be the only thing to link him to the murder." I said, "We're not through with you yet. I'll be back to talk to you later."

He said very sarcastically, "I'll be waiting for you."

I found Agent Jones waiting on the side of the house. I called to him and he came to the front. I asked him, "Did you find anything?"

He said, "Not a thing. How about you?"

I said, "I didn't find anything that might link him to the crime. Of course he denied everything about it. I did keep his registration. I think he got rid of the car."

"He probably dumped it into one of the lakes around here. It's probably sitting on the bottom of a lake," Agent Jones said.

"You really think he might have done this?"

He gave me a look like I was stupid or something. He said, "These people might come across as being dumb, but they're not. They have had a lot of practice avoiding the law. They know how to get away with things down here. Get used to it. This is going to be an uphill battle."

I was starting to understand why Agent Jones had been so pessimistic about the outcome of the case. Every time we took a small step forward, we ended up taking a few giant steps backwards. No one was willing to help us and put their life on the line. No one, black or white, wanted to talk to us. It seemed the case might end up as another murder statistic, but I didn't want it to happen.

We left and headed back to Reverend Jackson's house. We started talking about the case.

Agent Jones said, "You know he's going to tell Sheriff Crawford we paid him a little visit."

I said, "Probably."

"And probably nobody is going to talk to us now."

I said, "Agent Jones, you have such little faith in me."

He laughed and said, "It's not you I don't have faith in. It's the justice system down here in the good old South that I don't have faith in."

We arrived at Reverend Jackson's house and Agent Jones got out of the car. I stayed in the car and told him, "Go in the house. I will be right back."

He asked, "Where the hell are you going?"

I said, "I'm going to see good old Sheriff Crawford. I need to speak to him about something."

Agent Jones peered his head in the open window and said, "You be careful."

I said, "Don't worry, I will."

I headed straight for the center of town where the sheriff's office was located. When I flung open the door there was no Deputy Hank, so I walked over to the sheriff's door and opened it. What a surprise! No one was there either. I decided to take a chance go through his desk drawers and filing cabinets. I didn't care if I was breaking the law. I had a feeling he was hiding something.

While I was going through the cabinet. I heard someone coming in. I quickly shut the cabinet drawer and sat down in the chair that faced the sheriff's desk. Suddenly, the door flew open. I turned around and it was Sheriff Crawford.

He said, "What the hell are you doing in my office?"

I replied, "I saw the door was open, so I just walked in. I was just waiting until you came back."

He said, "I don't give two shits that you're a government agent. I could get you for trespassing."

I laughed and told him, "Go ahead, I would like that."

He threw his hat across the room and it landed on a chair in the corner. He asked, "Now what do I owe this visit to?"

I asked him, "Has anyone filed a report about a stolen car?"

He replied, "No, I don't think so, but let me check my records." He sat there a few seconds and then said, "No, I don't think anyone filed a report on a stolen car. Do you have any more questions that I can answer?"

I said, "No, that's all for now."

Before I left, he said, "Agent Pierce, I don't like you harassing the people of my town, especially accusing them of a crime like murder. I might just take offense to something like that."

I said, "Is that a threat, Sheriff Crawford? I don't take to kindly to threats."

He replied, "No, just a little advice. If you're going to accuse someone of a crime, you better have the evidence to back it up."

I said, "Don't worry, I'll have the evidence."

He just shook his head and laughed.

Agent Jones is right. These people might come across as backwards and little on the stupid side, but they aren't. They seem to be one step ahead of you. These people are very devious and cunning. It seems that you can't talk to anyone without it coming back to Sheriff Crawford.

I had a feeling that Sheriff Crawford knew who did it

and was covering up the crime. *Just a bunch of good old boys looking out for one another. Even when it comes to murder.*

I returned to Reverend Jackson's house a little pissed off. Time was running out to solve the crime and get the ones who committed it put in jail. The only credible witness was Reverend Jackson and I wasn't sure if he would be willing to testify. He still had to live in the town.

I walked into the house. Agent Jones was on the couch watching the television. I walked over and sat next to him.

I asked him, "What are you watching?"

He said, "The news."

I started to watch it with him They were showing a civil rights march in Birmingham, Alabama. One minute people were marching and then suddenly all hell broke loose. People were running everywhere. Big guard dogs attacked people and the police were beating them. Water from fire hoses was aimed and sprayed at people. It was a horrible sight.

"Even when we are peaceful and try to stand up for our rights, still something happens," Agent Jones said.

What can I say? I thought. I said nothing.

Reverend Jackson and his wife came in to the living room. Mrs. Jackson seemed to be glad to see me.

"I'm so happy you came back," she said. "Can I get you anything to drink or eat?"

I said, "No, thanks." She went into the kitchen.

Reverend Jackson sat down in a chair near us. He said, "It's such a pity that the world has to see this."

Agent Jones turned to me and aid, "Did you know Reverend Jackson participated in a civil rights march?"

I said, "Really, Reverend Jackson?"

Agent Jones said, "Go on, Reverend, tell him about it."

The reverend said, "Oh, I don't think he wants to hear about it."

I said, "No, please tell me, I'd like to hear about it."

Reverend Jackson told me, "Well, about forty of us boarded this bus. We were going to a march in Montgomery, Alabama. We were all so excited. I had heard that there were people coming from all over the United States. It wasn't just black folks that were going to march, it was white folks too. We all met at this one place. It was at this huge park. There must have been thousands of us. They came from different church congregations from all over. All different religions. We started marching down the main street in Montgomery. There were police all over the place. There were hundreds all on both side of us. I thought maybe they were protecting us from the angry white mob of people from the city. All of sudden, things started to go wrong. Some in the white mob lunged towards us. All hell broke loose. Things were flying. People were getting hit. Some in the march started to retaliate. Things went from bad to worse. Then the police stepped in. They just started swinging their clubs. They didn't care who they hit. I ended up getting hit in the head. I was bleeding a little, but I was all right. I was more worried about the people who were lying in the streets. I thought I'd better help them. I did what I could. The police started to arrest people on both sides. That's about it."

I was stunned. I had lived in New York for all my life. Such things didn't happen there. But here in the South, it happened every day. I was beginning to understand why Agent Jones felt the way he did. I wanted even more to catch the people who murdered the young boy.

Reverend Jackson got up and headed for the kitchen. I remained seated next to Agent Jones.

He asked, "How did things go with Sheriff Crawford?"

I said, "The same as always. I know he's hiding something. He knows more than he's telling us."

Agent Jones replied, "Oh, you think so?

I said, "Even though the word is out about us, I still want to talk to more people."

I didn't want to tell Agent Jones, but I found something in Pernel Williams' house. It was a piece of paper with some names and times written on it. *Could these be the others who were involved?* I wondered.

I decided to talk to whoever these people were. I asked Mrs. Jackson, "Do you have a phone book? Maybe I can find the name and look for the address."

I had two names, Andrew Whittaker and Joseph Fuller, but I didn't have addresses. Checking the phone book I hoped there would only be one or maybe two Whittakers and Fullers. To my surprise, there were three Andrew Whittakers and four Joseph Fullers.

Which one could it be? I pretty much gave up. *What if I talk to the wrong one? The right Andrew Whittaker or Joseph Fuller could end up leaving town and then we would have nothing.* I decided to keep the paper just in case.

I needed to go back to Pernel Williams' house, so I called the Atlanta field office and asked for more agents. They sent me two to do a more thorough search of the house.

Agent Jones stayed behind while myself and the other agents went to the house. I knocked on the door.

As usual, Mr. Williams staggered to the door. He said, "What the hell do you want now?"

I said, "I told you, Mr. Williams, that I wasn't done with you and I would be back."

He replied, "Get the hell off my property! You're trespassing. What gives you the right to bother me?"

I held up a search warrant that I had before. I said, "See this, Mr. Williams? This give me the right."

He opened the door and I entered the house. I told the other agents. "Check and look in every crack in this house."

I started searching the house. I went through drawers and looked under things. If there was something there, it would be to hard to find it with all the junk he had everywhere. I wanted something to tie him to the murder, anything, no matter what. I needed to find something that linked him to it. Any little bit of information.

I had been searching for about ten minutes when one of the agents came back with some pictures he had found in a drawer. The pictures were of three guys fishing. One was Pernel Williams.

I asked, "Mr. Williams, who are these other gentlemen in this picture with you?"

He said, "Let me see." I showed him the picture. He said. "They're nobody, just some fishin' friends."

I said, "I think they're more than fishing friends. Who are they?"

He replied, "I don't have to tell you nothin'. Why don't you arrest me?"

I said, "Don't worry, that time will come." I decided to keep the picture.

We tore the house apart, but the picture was the only thing we found. *Maybe the other two are Andrew Whittaker and Joseph Fuller.*

Now that I had a picture, I thought it would be a process of elimination. I decided to visit each of the Andrew Whittakers and Joseph Fullers. Maybe one would resemble the persons in the picture.

I told the other agents, "Go back to Atlanta until we need you again." Even though I would have liked them to stay in town, I thought it would be better if they went back. I feared that if the people of the town saw too many agents running around, they would react badly. We'd already had a hard enough time trying to get information out of them.

I went back to the Jacksons' house. I rushed in the door looking for Agent Jones, who was upstairs working on some paperwork.

I said, "I found a picture with Pernel Williams and a few of his friends." I gave it to Agent Jones to look at.

He looked at it and gave it back. He said, "It couldn't hurt to check them out."

I told him the names of who I thought the other were in the picture. "There's a little problem. There are a couple Andrew Whittakers and Joseph Fullers in town. We are going to have to pay a visit to each one and use the process of elimination."

He said, "If that's what we have to do, that's what we have to do."

I said, "Great, first thing tomorrow morning we go and do some visiting. I'm going to call the field office and try to get some more search warrants issued."

We got up pretty early. After talking to our people, I wanted to check out the lakes around town. We hadn't found the car at Pernel Williams' and if we didn't find it at the houses we were going to visit, I agreed they might have ditched it in one of the three lakes near the town. I told Agent Jones about it.

He said, "If you want to we can, but I'm telling you, you're not going to find it."

I thought he was being pessimistic and negative as usual. We had to find something to break open the case and we had to do it soon.

I received a call from our field office in Atlanta. They were told by the higher-ups at the FBI headquarters in D.C. that we had only three weeks to wrap the case up. We would then be recalled and reassigned. I decided not to tell Agent Jones. He already felt discouraged and I didn't want to add fuel to the fire.

Our first visit was to an Andrew Whittaker who lived at 323 Thomas Drive. I went up to the front door and knocked. An elderly gentleman came to the door. He looked at us dressed in our suits and said, "I don't want to buy nothin' so please leave."

I said, "Are you Andrew Whittaker?"

He said, "Yeah, who wants to know?"

I said, "We're not here to sell you anything. We are agents from the FBI. We need to speak to you for a minute."

I could tell he was not the Andrew Whittaker we were looking for. The one in the picture was half the man's age. I took the picture out of my coat pocket and gave it to him.

I asked him, "Do any of these men look familiar to you?"

The expression on his face when he looked at the picture told me that someone was familiar, but he said, "No, I never seen them before."

I was not going to play the game. I said, "I think you do and I'm not leaving until you tell me. I'm going right over there and sit in that chair until you tell me." I proceeded to walk over to a chair on his front porch.

I was about to sit in it when he said, "All right. I do recognize one of them. This is one." He pointed to one of the men in the photo. "That's my son."

I said, "Who are the others?"

"Well, I think this one is Joseph Fuller. He hangs around with my son, but the other one I don't know."

This is great. Now, we are getting somewhere. I said, "Thank you for your time."

I walked to the car where Agent Jones was waiting. I didn't care if he didn't recognize the others.

Agent Jones asked, "Did you get anywhere with him?"

I said, "Yes, I think things are going to start falling into place now." *We might have three of the four people who might have been in the car that night. Still, we have nothing on the fourth. Who is he? How is he involved?*

We needed to find the car. I wanted to go to the lakes and then interview the two other suspects later. I wanted to find the car and I wanted to find it bad.

I drove to the first lake, which was about five miles from the center of town. It wasn't very big. I parked alongside of it. Of course, Agent Jones insisted that I wasn't going to find anything. I wanted to prove him wrong. I walked to the edge of the lake and started to undress.

Agent Jones asked, "What the hell are you doing?"

I said, "I need to know if the car is in there. We don't have time to get people down here to drag the lake."

I was down to my boxers. I waded in a little ways and then started to walk to the center of the lake. It was pretty cold. The water wasn't very clear either, in fact, it was pretty murky. I couldn't even see my hand in the water.

I was practically at the center of the lake. My feet were touching the bottom and my head was still above water. I started back to the shore. I had a hard time getting back on the grass and Agent Jones helped pull me out.

He said, "I hope you're satisfied."

I said, "This lake is too shallow. We're not going to find a car in there." Agent Jones just shook his head. I decided not to get dressed and told him, "You drive to the next lake."

The second lake was a smaller than the first. I told Agent Jones, "We might as well drive to the third one. The third one may be the charm."

He just shook his head in disgust. I didn't care. We needed to look under every and any stone.

The third lake was a huge one. It was at least ten times

bigger than the other two. I wasn't able to walk right out in the center, so I walked down to the edge of the lake and dove into the water. I came up and went down again. I heard Agent Jones yelling from the edge of the lake, but I didn't care. I wanted to find the car.

I kept at it for a while and I was getting tired and out of breath. I started to make my way back to the edge of the lake. When I tried to get out of the water Agent Jones put out his hand to help, but I pushed it away.

I said, "Leave me alone, I don't need your help." I gathered up my clothes and started to walk towards a wooded area.

Agent Jones asked, "Where the hell are you going?"

I said, "I'm going to think, so don't bother me."

He said, "I'm telling you, these people aren't stupid. They know we could probably drag and dredge the lake and find the car. They're not going to dump it here."

I tried to ignore what he said. I just started walking straight for a heavily wooded area. Agent Jones headed back to the car.

We need that car, I thought. *Maybe Agent Jones is right. Maybe it is useless to waste so much time looking for the car. It could be halfway across the country or maybe they chopped it up into little pieces. But maybe, just maybe, we might get lucky and find it.*

I was about to return to the car when I noticed something odd in the distance. It looked like someone had made a kind of structure out of tree branches, maybe a child had built a fort of some kind. I walked over to it. As I got closer, I saw that it looked like someone had tried to cover something. I dropped my clothes on the ground and walked over to it. I started to remove the branches.

I nearly crapped in my underwear at what I saw. It was burnt-out shell of a car. I yelled, "Jones, Agent Jones, come here, I need your help, hurry." I couldn't control my excitement. I began to tremble a little.

Agent Jones came dashing through the woods. He said out of breath, "What the hell is it?"

I said, "Look over here." I pointed towards the object.

He had a shocked look on his face as he walked over to it. He touched it with his hand.

I asked, "Does this look like it could have been a station wagon?"

He said, "Yes, I think it was a station wagon at one time."

I turned to Agent Jones and said, "You were right, they didn't dump it in the lake. The bastards burnt it beyond recognition."

I started to walk around the car. I thought, *We've found the car or what's left of it. To come this far, only to find this.*

I was somewhat disappointed as I started to get dressed I walked around the car again and suddenly I saw something. I asked Agent Jones, "Do you have a penknife handy?"

He said, "No."

I told him, "Go back to the car and see if you can find a screwdriver with a flat end."

He asked, "What the hell are you doing?"

I said, "Just get me the screwdriver, for Christ sake."

He went back to the car while I looked at the car smiling now.

When he returned, he said, "I couldn't find a screwdriver with a flat end. The only thing I could find with a flat end is this crowbar."

I said, "That will do fine."

Agent Jones asked, "What are you doing?"

I said, "They might have burnt the car so we couldn't distinguish what kind of car it was or what the color was.

They forgot one thing, the vehicle identification number plate in the front of the car."

Agent Jones asked, "What are you talking about?"

I said, "Every car model, no matter what car company it comes from, has a vehicle identification number. All we have to do is look up what company uses these numbers and we can determine the make, the model, the year and the color, who owned it."

It took me some time, but I was able to pry the plate off. I turned around and said to Agent Jones, "They're not as smart as they think they are."

We went back to Reverend Jackson's house and gathered all our evidence together. It wasn't much, but it was coming together. All we needed was to turn up the heat on our suspects and put more pressure on them. Our mission the next day was to interview Joseph Fuller and Andrew Whittaker, Jr. Although we had circumstantial evidence, I thought we might have enough to make an arrest. Agent Jones wasn't so sure.

Five

First we went to see Joseph Fuller. I had a feeling he would lie to us like everyone else had so far, but we still needed to talk to him. I had his address and we drove to his home located down a long dirt road. There were a lot of abandoned houses on each side. For people who thought they were better than others, they certainly didn't live that way.

I found the house. There was a big bloodhound in the front yard barking his head off. I had Agent Jones distract the dog while I made a mad dash to the front door. Lucky for me, the dog was chained. I knocked on the door. A young woman holding a baby came to the door.

I asked her, "May I speak to your husband, Joseph Fuller?"

She said, "He ain't my husband. He's my boyfriend."

I said, "Whoever he is, could I speak with him?"

She said, "He went out with his boys about an hour ago."

I replied back, "Do you know when he'll be back?"

She said, "You got me."

I thought about waiting for him to return when suddenly the woman came out the door and stood on the steps. She said, "What's he done now?"

I asked, "What do you mean, what's he done now?"

She said, "You're the law ain't ya?"

I said, "Sort of."

She replied, "He's always getting into some kind of trouble. What is it now? It's nothin' really bad is it?"

I didn't answer her questions, but said, "I'll sit on the steps here a while and wait for him."

She said, "Can I offer you somethin' to drink? I got some Coca-Cola."

I said, "No, thank you, ma'am."

She went back into the house. I decided to wait on the steps. Agent Jones was waiting in the car, just in case we needed to leave quickly.

I got up and looked at my watch. I had been waiting a good half-hour. I was about to leave when I saw a man walking with two small children towards us. He spotted me and slowed his pace. He kept walking towards me while the children walked ahead of him. He walked past the car and looked at it then came up the front walk to the house. The dog started barking loudly and running around in circles.

He yelled out to the dog, "Duke, Duke, stop that damn barking!"

He walked toward me. He was short and stocky. He looked to be in his early thirties. He was missing a few teeth.

I asked, "Are you Joseph Fuller?"

He replied, "Yeah, that's me. Who wants to know?"

I said, "I think you better send your kids inside."

He turned to his kids and yelled, "Jimmy, Joe Junior, get in the house." One of the kids whined and asked why. He replied, " 'Cause I told you to."

He asked, "What do you need to talk to me about?"

I told him, "We are investigating the murder of Nathaniel Johnson."

He said, "I don't know nothin' about that."

I said, "I think you do." I continued. "If you cooperate with us, you won't have any problems. If you don't and you lie to us, you're going to be in a helluva lot of trouble."

77

He looked like he wanted to tell me something by the look on his face. I waited for an answer.

He started to talk again. "Like I said before, I don't know nothin' about it."

I said, "Fine. I'm leaving now for the time being, but I'm coming back with a search warrant and I'm going to turn your house upside down." I got into the car.

Agent Jones drove. He asked, "Did he tell you anything?"

I said, "No, but I think he wants to. He looked like he wanted to. I think we need to be more forceful. We need to apply more pressure."

Agent Jones replied, "Do you think that's going to help?"

I said, "Well, it can't hurt. I think now they know we're onto them. Maybe one of them will get scared and rat on the others. I'm hoping for that. Our next appointment is with Andrew Whittaker, Junior."

We drove straight to his home. Agent Jones turned to me. "I have a feeling that Mr. Whittaker is already going to know we're coming."

I replied, "I'm afraid you're right."

Joseph Fuller and Andrew Whittaker lived close to each other. Their houses were less than a mile apart, so it took us almost no time to get there.

Before we could though, Andrew Whittaker was standing in the road.

I asked Agent Jones, "Stop the car. Stay here, if something should happen, I want you to go back and get help."

He said, "I don't think I can do that, we're in this together."

I said, "As your superior, I order you to stay in the car."

He laughed and said, "You're not my superior." I thought I would try anyway.

We both got out I walked a little ahead of Agent Jones.

Mr. Whittaker yelled, "Get away from my property and take that nigger boy with you."

I said, "Now, Mr. Whittaker, there's no need to talk like that. I just need to ask a few questions."

He said, "The only way you're going to ask me a few questions is if you tie me up and beat the answer out of me."

I replied, "That could be arranged."

He said, "You think you're real funny, don't you? Why don't you leave us alone? Making a fuss over some little nigger boy."

I saw in the corner of my eye that Agent Jones was getting closer to me. He didn't look happy. I was afraid something might happen. I turned around and whispered to him, "Don't pay attention to what he's saying. He's baiting you. He wants you to do something. Don't give him the satisfaction."

Agent Jones backed off a little. I continued talking to Mr. Whittaker. "Could we go some place and discuss this like gentlemen?"

Mr. Whittaker said, "I ain't discussing nothing. There ain't nothing to discuss. Now I want both of you off my property and to leave me and my family alone."

I said, "I can't do that. I'm here to investigate a crime. That's my job and I'm going to do it."

He said, "It's going to be pretty hard for you to do your job if you're dead."

Suddenly, he pulled out a gun.

I said very calmly, "You're not thinking of shooting me, are you? Especially with a witness."

He said "I'll shoot him too."

I said, "I don't think so. If you shoot me, then my partner will have to shoot you. Then he'll have to go to the authorities and you will be charged with my murder."

He replied "Nobody is going to believe some nigger over me, even if he is with the law."

I told him, "You have ten seconds to put the gun away or my partner is going to shoot you."

He said, "He ain't got the guts."

Agent Jones put his gun and hand on my shoulder, pointing it at Mr. Whittaker.

I said, "I'm going to count to ten and my partner, Mr. Jones, is going to shoot you." I started counting. "One, two, three, four . . . When I got to seven, he dropped the gun.

I was glad it was over because I thought we might have to shoot him. I hoped not. I thought, *What if he's the killer? Everything we have worked for so far will crumble right before us.*

Agent Jones and I walked over to him. Agent Jones still had his gun cocked ready to fire. I walked over, grabbed the gun, took out the bullets and threw them in the grass. I decided to keep the gun.

I said to him, "We're going now, but we're coming back here and you can be sure of that."

As we walked away, Mr Whittaker let out a huge wad of spit that hit Agent Jones in the face. I thought, *Oh, shit!*

Before I could move, Agent Jones lunged at him. He grabbed Whittaker around the neck and was ready to bash his face in with his fist. I grabbed his arm before he could hit him.

I said, "No, Jones, don't do it. It would be a waste of your energy."

He pulled his arm back hard from my hand. He then let go of Mr. Whittaker's neck. He took out his handkerchief and wiped his face.

I told him, "Get back in the car."

He walked back to the car. I grabbed Mr. Whittaker by the scruff of his neck.

I said, "You're nothing but a low-life piece of white

trash. I should have let him tear you apart. You better be glad I stopped him, but you know there's nothing stopping me. You know what, you're not even worth the energy in thinking about it."

We got back into our car and left. I was relieved that it was over. I thought Agent Jones was going to lose it. I said to him, "I'm glad you had some self-control out there. God knows what might have happened."

Agent Jones replied, "You don't know how much I wanted to shoot him."

I said, "I'm glad you didn't. There goes our whole case up in smoke."

Agent Jones asked, "What did you say to him after I came back to the car?"

"Oh, I told him how much I thought he was such an upstanding citizen in the community."

He laughed and said, "I bet you did."

My nerves were a little shattered. I told Agent Jones, "I need a drink. I think you need one too. I think we might go back to that place we ate lunch that one day."

It was about five in the evening when we walked in the restaurant. Joline, our waitress and hostess from the last time, was there.

She said, "Well, look what the cat dragged in. It's the two good-looking lawmen. What can I do you boys for?"

Agent Jones said, "We're here for some dinner."

She said, "Well, just follow me and I'll get you guys started. Do you men want anything to drink?"

Agent Jones said, "I'd like a beer."

I needed something stronger. "I'll take a glass of gin straight up."

Joline gave me a look and said, "Well, it looks like someone had a hard day." She smiled and said, "You men sit tight, your drinks will be coming."

I told Agent Jones, "Don't order for me. I want to look at a menu first."

The menu had some unusual dishes. Something called hushpuppies, which I always thought were a make of shoes. Deep-fried pork chops. Some of the things I couldn't even pronounce.

I decided on the fried chicken with mashed potatoes and green beans. Agent Jones had the deep-fried pork chops with mashed potatoes and collard greens. I said, "You going to eat those things again."

He said, "They're great, you don't know what you're missing."

I said, "I can live with that."

Joline brought our drinks right over. I needed it to unravel my nerves. It was all right to talk and laugh about what happened, but it could have taken a bad turn. We could have had a major incident, especially if Agent Jones had struck that piece of scum. He could have been arrested for assault. I couldn't stop thinking about it.

We had finished our dinner. I wanted to make our way back to Reverend Jackson's house. I decided to drive because Agent Jones had a few beers and I didn't trust him driving. I'd only had the one drink.

I started back to the Reverend Jackson's house. Agent Jones decided to lay back and sleep. It was a rough day and I just wanted to get back to the house.

Finally when we arrived at the house, I had to shake Agent Jones to wake him up. He seemed a little groggy as he said, "What, what do you want?"

I said, "We're back home."

He wiped both of his eyes and got out of the car. We had

been at Reverend Jackson's house for almost a week. I felt we were imposing and might be overstaying our welcome.

I thought, *Maybe we should look for some place to rent until we conclude this case.*

Agent Jones decided to go to bed. I stayed downstairs because I wanted to talk to Mrs. Jackson, who just came out of the kitchen.

She said, "Where have you men been? It's past seven. I kept your dinner warmed."

I felt bad. I didn't have the heart to tell her we had already eaten. I told her, "You shouldn't have done that."

She said, "Oh, it's not a problem. I always cook like I'm feeding an army, so I don't mind."

I told her, "I'm not that hungry, but I will eat a little."

She asked about Agent Jones. "Doesn't Franklin want anything to eat?"

I said, "No, Franklin is not feeling too well. I think he'll probably pass up dinner tonight."

She brought a plate out that was piled with pieces of roast beef with carrots and potatoes. It was just too much to eat, but I tried anyway.

I told her, "I need to talk to you about something."

She asked, "What is it, Daniel?"

I said, "I think it would be better if we leave you and Mr. Jackson."

She said with a surprised look on her face, "Why?"

I told her, "I believe we are wearing out our welcome and that maybe you think we are taking advantage of you."

She said, "Why would you think that? Otis and I love having you both here. Neither one of you is a bother. Anyway, we feel so much safer with you here."

I said, "That's another reason. I think me and Agent Jones are putting you at risk being here. I'm afraid someone might try something."

She looked at me and grabbed my hand and said, "Listen dear, Otis and I have been through a lot. We have had anything and everything done to us. We're still here. We're going to still be here after you're gone, so don't worry."

Even though she was trying to make me feel good and reassure me, I was still worried. She was such a sweet woman, I didn't think I could bear anything or anyone harming her.

She looked down at my plate and said, "You were right, you weren't very hungry."

I said, "I feel bad that you wasted it."

She said, "Oh, it's not wasted, I'll put it in the ice box and Otis will eat it tomorrow."

I decided it was time to go to bed as well. I slowly walked up the steps and down the hallway into the room. I got undressed and then made a quick trip to the bathroom. I washed up a little before going to bed. I tried to be very quiet because I thought that Agent Jones was asleep.

I got into bed and pulled the sheet on top of me. Suddenly, I heard someone say something. It was Agent Jones. I turned over to face his bed.

He said, "Hey, Pierce, are you asleep?"

I said, "No, not yet."

He said, "Thanks for not getting mad at me earlier today."

I asked, "What do you mean?"

He said, "You know, when I went after Andrew Whittaker, thanks for understanding."

I said, "Well, he did spit on you. I think I might have done the same if he had spit on me."

We continued talking. I said, "I know you wanted to kill him. I was thinking if I wasn't there you might have."

He replied, "You might be right, I was really angry at that moment."

I told him, "Whatever is bothering you, you have to let it

out and let go of it. It's going to hurt you as an agent. You have to have self-control in this job. You have to let things fall by the wayside."

He said, "I think you're right about that."

I was about to try to go to sleep when I heard Agent Jones saying something again. I said, "Did you say something to me, Jones?"

He said, "Yeah, I asked you why you don't call me by my first name, Franklin."

I told him, "I guess out of respect. You're Agent Jones and I'm Agent Pierce."

He replied, "I do have a first name. It's Franklin. Can't you call me Franklin'?"

I said, "All right, from now on I will refer to you as Agent Franklin. Are you happy now?"

He said, "Yes, I am, Agent Daniel."

"Remember when you said to me I could tell you anything?" Agent Franklin said.

"Yeah, I remember."

He said, "You said you wanted to know why I act and feel the way I do. I'm going to tell you why. You might not like what I'm about to say."

I thought, *What's he going to tell me? Maybe he doesn't even like me because I'm white.* I was sort of afraid of what I was about to hear.

Agent Jones told me his story. "Remember when I told you about my mother sending me to Chicago to live with my aunt?"

I said, "Yes, I remember."

"Well, I didn't tell you why."

I said, "I thought it was because your mother thought you would have a better life in the north."

He said, "Well, that's not the whole story."

Agent Jones had piqued my interest, so I said to him, "Continue."

He said, "You see, my father just didn't die. He was murdered." I was shocked. He continued, "You see, for blacks, life was very hard in the South. It was also hard for the whites. No jobs, no future, especially during the Depression." He stopped for a few seconds.

I asked him, "Why did you stop?"

He didn't say anything for awhile then he continued. "There was this mine. They would mine kaolin and granite. They only hired whites to work there. There was a strike by the white workers. The mine owners decided to bring in black miners to replace them. They could pay them less anyway."

Suddenly, he stopped again. I wondered, *Why did he stop?*

He said, "I'm sorry, it's hard for me to talk about this."

I asked, "Do you want to stop?"

He said, "No, you asked me and I'm going to tell you,." He continued with his story. "My father and other blacks started to work in the mine. Every time they entered the gates of the mine, they were spit at and had things thrown at them as the trucks that brought them in went by. One day my father and some of the people he worked with decided to go out together. They decided to stay on the black side of the town and went to a bar. Someone had spotted them at this bar. Someone white who used to work at the mines before the strike. Word got back to the white mine workers who were out of jobs. They loaded up some trucks and cars and drove to the other side of town. They surrounded the building. My father and his friends couldn't get out. They decided they would have to fight their way out. A huge brawl ensued. Men on both sides were fighting with their fists and then weapons. The whole thing lasted about ten minutes. After it was over, there were four men dead. One was white, three were black. One of them was my father. They had beaten him so bad, he was unrecognizable."

He looked at me and shook his head back and forth. He said, "The funniest thing was that all the blacks who fought back that night were hauled in and charged with all these crimes. Some were charged with murder. Not one white was arrested or charged. Can you understand why I feel the way I feel sometimes?"

I walked over and put my hand on his shoulder. He looked up at me and smiled. I said, "We better get some sleep, it's going to be a long day tomorrow."

Six

When I awoke the next morning, Agent Jones was already gone. I don't think he got very much sleep during the night. I got up and took my shower.

As usual, when I walked downstairs, Mr. Jackson had breakfast ready for me to eat. I looked around but I didn't see Franklin anywhere.

I asked Mrs. Jackson, "Do you know where Agent Jones is?"

She said, "No, he must have gotten up early and left. I haven't seen him since I was down here."

Suddenly, someone walked in the door. It was Agent Jones. I said, "I was wondering what happened to you."

He said, "I couldn't sleep much last night, so I got up early and took a walk."

I felt bad about making Franklin tell me about what happened to his father. It must have been like opening up an old wound that had healed.

I asked him, "How do you feel?"

He said, "I'm fine. You don't have to worry about me. I'll be fine."

I did worry about Franklin's state of mind though. I never knew what might set him off.

I needed to make a call to the field office in Atlanta. I wanted to tell them that we were gathering a lot of evidence and might be able to make an arrest soon. Of course, I was being overly optimistic. We needed a huge break. We needed someone to slip up and say something that they shouldn't. I thought that Agent Jones and I should be relentless in our pursuit, almost to the point of harassment. Maybe then one of them would break.

I made my call. I told them about what had happened. Our commander wanted to see me back in Atlanta. I asked him, "Why?"

He wouldn't tell me. I didn't understand, but I was told not to bring Agent Jones with me. Again I asked, "Why?"

He told me, "Leave him there and just come to Atlanta alone. Make an excuse and leave him there."

Something is up, but what?

I got off the phone. He could tell by the look on my face that something was wrong. Agent Jones asked, "What's the matter?"

I said, "It's nothing. I need to go back to Atlanta."

He said, "I'll go up and get changed."

I said, "No, you're not going."

He had a surprised look on is face. He asked, "Why not?"

I had to make something up. I hated lying to him. I believe that he finally trusted me and now I had to tell him a bold face lie.

I said, "Atlanta wants you to stay here and watch the Jacksons. They're worried that they might be harmed."

He replied, "How would they know this?"

I told him, "It's confidential." I think he knew I wasn't telling the truth, but I finally talked him into staying with them while I went back to Atlanta.

I was back in Atlanta at the field office. Commander Holden wanted to see me right away. I walked into his office he looked up from his desk and told me, "Sit down."

I sat down while Commander Holden went through

some papers on his desk. I had to wait a few minutes before he finished.

He looked up from his desk and said, "I'm thinking of calling Agent Jones back to the field office and replacing him. I don't think he has the mindset or the patience in doing his job. But before I replace him, I want to hear your opinion."

I looked at the commander and told him flat out, "Sir, you can't replace him now. He's done so much in getting the information we need to build this case. If you replace him now, all the time would have been wasted."

He squinted his eyes and gave me a look. He said "All right, I won't replace him yet, but you better keep a tighter leash on him."

I got up from my chair and smiled. I put out my hand to shake the commander's. He put his hand out and smiled back. He repeated what he said earlier.

I replied, "I'll do whatever I have to do. I won't let anything ruin what we both have accomplished so far."

It was almost time to leave and I didn't really like what I had heard. Somehow they had found out that Agent Jones assaulted someone. They didn't mention names, but I knew. I had a feeling that Sheriff Crawford had something to do with it. Even though I thought Agent Jones was justified in what he had done, they didn't.

I had to drive all the way back to Miner's Bluff. I probably wouldn't make it until sometime after nine. I really didn't feel like going back. If they were thinking of taking him off the case, they would have to tell him themselves. I wasn't saying a word. I was finally gaining his trust and we were starting to come together as partners. There was no way in hell I was going to tell him.

It seemed like it took forever to get back. I was sleepy as I had already had a full day. I made my way to the reverend's house. From a distance, I could see what looked to be smoke. I stepped on the gas pedal and drove as fast as I could. As I got closer, the smoke became thicker.

I jumped out of the car and headed for the house. I saw a few people running around and ran over to where they were. They had buckets of water and were trying to put the fire out. Others had tree branches doing the same.

I looked at the people, but I didn't recognize any of them. I started to look for Agent Jones, but didn't see him anywhere. Suddenly, I heard someone call my name and turned around. It was Mrs. Jackson. She ran towards me and I started to run to her.

She said, "Oh, Daniel! Oh, Daniel!" That was all she said.

I asked, "What happened?"

She said, "We all heard something hit the front of the house. We didn't know what it was. When we ran to see, there were these flames on the front porch. The swing had caught fire."

She started to weep uncontrollably. She said, "Why would they do this to us? We never bother anybody."

I tried to console her as much as I could. I asked her, "Where are the reverend and Agent Jones?"

She said, "Oh, Otis is in the house. He was trying to save our things and some of our mementos. About Franklin, he was here, but he took off. I don't know where. He took our car. I'm really worried about him. He was not thinking straight when he left."

I couldn't believe what was happening. After all I had gone through during the day, defending Agent Jones, and now he had gone off. The case and everything we'd worked so hard for was going to end if I didn't find him soon.

I asked Mrs. Jackson, "Are you all right?"

She said, "We'll be all right. You have to go find Franklin. I know he's going to get himself in a heap of trouble."

I decided to go straight to Andrew Whittaker's house. I had a feeling I would find Agent Jones there. I drove as fast as I could, praying that Agent Jones would not do something stupid.

It was hard driving at night as there were no lights. I was nearly blind and prayed that I didn't hit something or someone. I turned down the road where Andrew Whittaker's house was and started to slow down. I didn't want to alarm anyone.

I came to a stop. I didn't see Reverend Jackson's car anywhere. I got out of the car. I took my gun out and held it close to my side. I wasn't taking any chances. I walked towards the house but didn't see anything unusual. I looked around, but still didn't see Agent Jones.

I thought, *I wonder where he is? It seems he didn't come over here, so where is he?*

I decided to go over to Pernel Williams' house and then Joseph Fuller's. I didn't see Agent Jones at either place.

I thought, *Maybe he went someplace to let off some steam.* I hoped for the best, but expected the worst. I decided to make my way back to the Jacksons' house.

The fire was out when I got back. It had burned the outside porch and the front of the house, otherwise there wasn't a lot of damage. I walked inside the house and the smell of smoke was everywhere. I saw Reverend Jackson and his wife. I walked over to them.

"How are you two doing?"

Reverend Jackson said, "By the grace of God, we're still here. He was watching over us tonight."

Mrs. Jackson nodded in agreement. She said, "Franklin is upstairs. He came back a few minutes ago."

I ran up the steps and entered the room. He was sitting

on his bed. I was glad to see Agent Jones. I thanked God for not letting him do anything he would be sorry for.

I then said, "Where the hell were you? I've been looking everywhere for you. I thought you might do something stupid."

He looked up. He had a hurt look on his face. He said, "I would never do what you are thinking."

I said, "I'm not too sure of that. I still want to know where you were at."

He said, "I went to the church."

I said, "To the church?"

"To the church."

I was surprised by his answer. I'd been looking all over for him and thinking the worst and the whole time he was at the church.

He said, "Either I had to go there or I would have gone someplace else. I thought it was better if I went there."

I didn't ask where else he was. It was better that I didn't know. I asked him, "Are you all right?"

He said, "Yeah, I guess I'm all right. I was a little scared. I felt bad for the Jacksons. They have been so nice to the both of us. What about Atlanta? What did headquarters want?"

What am I going to tell him? I needed to make something up and hope he would believe me. I told him, "It was nothing. Just a lot of bureaucratic garbage." I wasn't going to say anything to him, so I told him, "Get some sleep. I'm going back downstairs."

Reverend Jackson and his wife were both sitting in the kitchen. When I entered the kitchen, Mrs. Jackson was getting a coffeepot off the stove. She said, "Have a seat. I've made some fresh coffee. Do you want some?"

I said, "Yes, that would be nice." I needed it. "I think I better stay downstairs, just in case those idiots come back."

She said, "Oh, you don't have to do that. You need your sleep for your job."

I told her, "I will feel better if I do."

She shrugged her shoulders and said, "If that's what you want to do."

I told them, "Go to bed and try to sleep."

I knew it probably would be an impossible task. I watched them go upstairs. I decided to stay up a while, just in case. I cared a lot for these people and I was determined not to let anything happen to them, even if it meant having to take someone's life.

I felt someone shaking me. It was Agent Jones. He said, "I see you fell asleep on the job."

I couldn't believe it. I had promised them I would stay up and watch the house. I became annoyed with myself.

Franklin said, "Don't worry, you've only been asleep for about half an hour."

I told him, "I'm calling headquarters to get some more agents down here to guard the house."

He said, "Do you really think they're going to send any more men down here?"

I said, "Yes, after what I'm going to tell them. Reverend Jackson is our only witness who's willing to testify. Our whole case hinges on him. Do you think that they're going to let anything happen to him?"

He replied, "Truthfully, I don't know."

Mrs. Jackson, as usual, was downstairs making breakfast. Even after the previous night her schedule and mood did not change. It was like nothing had happened. I felt bad for the Jacksons. I felt responsible for what happened. Somehow they found out where we were staying. I believe they were trying to kill us, but instead nearly killed the Jacksons in the process. I felt we needed to leave.

I told Agent Jones, "We need to leave. We are endangering them if we stay here."

He said, "I feel the same way."

The phone rang. Mrs. Jackson got up to answer it. She stood for about a minute, without speaking.

I thought, *I wonder what is going on? Maybe it's a call threatening her and Mr. Jackson.*

She came back to the kitchen table with a puzzled look on her face.

I asked her, "What's the matter?"

She said, "That was the strangest phone call. They only gave me an address and time and told me to tell you to meet him there."

She gave me the address. It was Pernel Williams' residence. He wanted to meet us at seven in the evening. I felt a twinge of excitement go through me.

I thought, *Finally, one of them is breaking down under the pressure. Finally, this case might be near its conclusion.*

She asked me, "What's this about?"

I told her, "It's official business." I didn't want them involved any more than they already were.

Reverend Jackson came into the kitchen. I sat them both down at the table and told them, "We're leaving and won't be staying with you anymore."

Mrs. Jackson seemed very upset. She said, "It's not because of what happened last night, is it?"

I told her, "Yes, Agent Jones and I feel being here has put you at risk. I just don't want anything to happen to either of you."

She smiled and looked at us and said, "You two didn't have anything to do with what happened last night. Otis and I have been going through this kind of stuff for many years. We always dealt with it and came through it."

Even with her words of encouragement, I still thought it was best if we left.

I was about to leave the kitchen when Reverend Jackson said, "Wait a minute I know you're having problems with some of our people talking to you."

I said, "Yes, I have. You two are about the only ones who have been willing to speak to us."

He continued, "Well, after what happened last night, a couple of them want to talk to you. I don't think they know a lot, but still it might help you."

After what happened, things seemed to be looking up. I told Franklin what Reverend Jackson said. He said, "I hope we're not wasting our time."

I told him, "Any information, however small it is, will help us."

He said, "We've been down this road before. They might tell us what they know, but when it comes to proving it, we might have a problem."

I told Franklin, "Check out all the people Reverend Jackson knows who are willing to talk to us now. I am going to visit the boarding house I saw earlier to see if I can get a room. We need to get out of the Jackson's house, the sooner the better."

The boarding house was about ten miles out of town. It wasn't very big. I walked in the front door. It was run by an older black man and a woman who appeared to be his daughter. They gave me a strange look. I guess they wondered why I was there.

I walked over to them and said, "I'm a visitor here in town and I need a room to rent." They both gave me a strange look again.

The older black man said, "You know we rent to black folks."

I said, "I don't care. I just need to rent a room."

I think they were afraid of me. I guess no whites had ever wanted to rent a room before. I told them, "Look, I'm with my friend. You see, he's black. Most white-owned places won't rent to me when they find out that I'm with my friend, who is black."

The young woman looked at her father and said, "Well, Daddy, I don't see why we can't rent a room to him. As long as he got money to pay for it." She looked at me and said, "You got money to pay for it, don't you?"

I said, "Yes, I do." I pulled out my wallet and showed her.

She said, "Well, alright then." She gave me a card to fill out. She said, "The room rent is twenty-five dollars a week."

I went back to the Jackson house and told the Jacksons and Agent Jones.

It was about 6:30 in the evening. I told Agent Jones, "We better make our way over to Pernel Williams' house."

We both loaded our guns just in case. Agent Jones took out another clip and put it in his coat jacket.

I asked him, "Why did you do that?"

He said, "You never know what's going to happen. I just want to be on the safe side."

I told him, "We are not going to provoke anything."

He just looked at me.

We started over to Pernel Williams' house. I was a bit nervous. Agent Jones and I didn't speak. I wasn't happy about the time as it would be getting dark soon. I didn't like the idea of being around there in the dark. We saw the sun was starting to set. The sky had an eerie blue, orange, and red look to it. I just wanted to get it over as quickly as possible.

I turned onto the road Pernel Williams lived. It was sort of eerie. I couldn't put my finger on it. It seemed so quiet and serene. I decided to park the car away from the house and walk the rest of the way. We both got out of the car. We both felt something strange in the air. Agent Jones walked round the car and stood next to me.

He said, "I don't like this. There's something strange going on here."

On our way down the road towards the house, we looked around. There was no one out in their yards and no dogs barking in the yards. I looked at the houses. All the windows were shut. I thought that was strange, being it was about 95 degrees out.

I turned to Agent Jones and said, "I don't like this at all. I think we better go back to the car."

We turned around and started to walk very quickly back to the car. We still had about fifty feet to go when I saw a car coming down the road fast and kicking up a lot of dust.

I told Agent Jones, "We better get back to the car and fast."

We started to run. Finally we were at our car, the other car was almost upon us.

Suddenly, I saw the muzzle of a gun. Before I could do anything, shots rang out. Agent Jones and I both shot back. When the car was even to ours, I ducked behind our car, grabbing Agent Jones by the coat collar and pulling him down with me. Some of the bullets busted our back windows and glass flew every which way. As the car passed us and went the road. I started to shoot again, but I only had one bullet left.

I knew Agent Jones had an extra clip. He was lying in a heap against the car. I thought maybe I had hurt him when I dragged him down behind the car.

I said to him, "I need your extra clip."

I opened his jacket to reach in his coat pocket. When I did. I saw blood forming on his white shirt. I looked at it for a few seconds. I took the clip and put it in my gun. The car was pretty far down the road. I stood in the middle of the road, aimed towards it and started to shoot. I kept on shooting until I didn't have any more bullets.

I ran back over to Agent Jones, picked him up, and put him in the car. I tried to be very careful because I didn't want to hurt him any more than he already was. He was bleeding badly and didn't say much. Anyway, I thought it was better if he didn't talk.

I said, "Don't worry, Franklin, I'm going to get you help. I need to find a hospital. I'm going to have to go back to Reverend Jackson's house. Maybe they can tell me where one is at."

As I drove, I took out my handkerchief and applied it to the area where he was bleeding. I told him, "Franklin hold this on your wound. It might slow down the bleeding."

He put his hand on it. I drove as fast as I could back to Reverend Jackson's house. Speeding and making quick turns, I thought I might end up killing us both.

We finally arrived back at the Jacksons' house and I ran inside. Mrs. Jackson was sitting on the sofa in the living room. She could tell by the look on my face something terrible had happened. She asked me, "What happened?"

I said, "Franklin has been shot. I need to get him to a hospital.

Suddenly, Mrs. Jackson, one who could be counted to be steady in a crisis, started to cry.

I told her, "You need to calm yourself. Where's the closest hospital?"

She told me, "Wilson Memorial Hospital. It's on Lavender Road."

I said, "Thanks for the information."

I ran out of the house. She seemed to want to tell me something else, but I didn't have time. I looked on a map that I had and found the road. It was about nine miles away. I looked down at Agent Jones. He didn't look good. He was losing a lot of blood. I told him everything would be all right. Still, I was afraid he might die before I got him to the hospital. I flew down the road.

It all seemed like a bad dream. Maybe I should have suspected something might be wrong. I thought, *I wonder why Pernel Williams wanted to see me so late? Whoever it was not only is going to be charged first-degree murder for killing Nathaniel Johnson, but also with attempted murder of two federal agents and if Agent Jones dies, another first degree murder. They'd planned this.*

I looked over at Agent Jones again. He seemed to be drifting in and out of consciousness. I saw a tall, somewhat white building come into view. I hoped it was the hospital. I made a hard left turn into the parking lot. I saw from the front that it was the hospital and drove straight up to the front doors. I got out and ran as fast as I could through the doors.

I saw a nurse behind a counter and ran over to her. "You got to help me, my partner's been shot. I think he might be bleeding to death. You've got to help him."

She said, "You have to calm down and tell me slowly." I repeated myself so she would understand me. She asked, "Where is he?"

I said, "He's in my car that's parked outside I didn't want to move him, just in case."

She walked from behind the counter and said, "Show me where he is."

I said, "Follow me." We walked out to the car. I said, "He's on the passenger side." I opened the car door.

Suddenly, the look on her face changed. She said, "I'll be back, you wait here."

I said to her, "Hurry please." I kept talking to Franklin.

I told him, "Everything is going to be all right. We made it to the hospital."

I must have waited for about five minutes. I thought, *What the hell is going on? I thought that she was going back in there to get some more people to help him out of the car.*

I started walking toward the door when I saw the nurse and a few other people coming towards me. One looked like a doctor. Everyone came outside.

I said, "What the hell are you all waiting for? What are you all standing around for?"

Finally the doctor spoke, "I'm sorry, sir, but we can't admit him to our hospital."

I said very loudly, "What do you mean you can't admit him? He's been shot. He's bleeding badly. He's going to die if you don't help now."

They just looked at each other.

The doctor spoke again. "We don't want any trouble, but we can't take him here."

I was furious. I started screaming, "Do you know what I am? I'm with the FBI. I'm part of the government. This is my partner. You can't refuse us. Who the hell do you think you are?"

The doctor walked back in the hospital. The nurse and two large men stayed outside. I said, "What is he doing?"

The nurse said, "He might be calling the police."

I thought, *What the hell is going on here?* I felt like I was in an episode of *The Twilight Zone.* I asked her, "Why are you refusing to admit him?"

She said, "You really want to know why?"

I said, "Yes."

She said, "We only accept whites at this hospital. Negroes aren't allowed. You can take him to the medical center that admits Negroes."

I asked her, "Where is it?"

She gave me directions. It was five miles away. I thought, *Franklin might not make it.*

I went up to the nurse and said, "You're all going to regret this. I don't care what color he is, you can't refuse him medical help. That's an oath you were supposed to have taken."

I couldn't believe what was happening. I drove as fast as I could to the other medical center. Agent Jones was no longer talking. I thought, *He might have just died on me.*

I kept talking to him, but he didn't answer back. The whole time, I thought about what he had told me—about his father and his family, his wife and two kids.

I finally arrived at the medical center. It was a one-story building. There didn't look like much to it. I walked in. People were sitting everywhere, every one of them black. As I walked in, the people stared at me. They probably wondered why I was there and if I was going to take one of them away. I felt very strange right then.

I walked over to a woman who was helping an elderly lady up from a chair. I said to her, "Are you a nurse? If you are, I need your help right this minute."

She said, "Sort of, actually, I'm a nurse's aid. If you could wait a minute. I would be willing to help you."

I told her, "I don't have a minute, I need your help now."

She handed the old woman off to someone else. She said, "What is it? If you're here to arrest someone, you're going to have wait until they're looked at."

I told her, "No, it's my friend he needs some medical attention."

She looked at me funny and said, "Sir, I don't know if you realize this, but you're at a place for black people. There's a hospital for whites that's a couple miles away that probably he would feel better being in." She could tell by the look on my face that I was desperate. She said, "All right, you can bring your friend in."

I said, "You're going to go out and get him. I don't think he's conscious."

She said, "Wait here. I'll go get a gurney for him." She returned with the gurney and two tall black men. She said, "Where is he?"

I said, "He's in the car."

We went out to the car. It was too dark out to see inside the car. When I opened the car door, the light came on. All three of them looked at each other.

The nurse said, "You didn't say he was a black man."

The two black men pulled Agent Jones out and put him on the gurney. The nurse started to check for vital signs.

She said, "His breathing is very shallow. He looks like he's lost a lot of blood."

They rushed him inside the center and took him into a back room. The nurse turned around and told me, "You wait here."

I walked over to where everyone else was sitting. I looked for a place to sit down, but there were no empty seats. Since I couldn't sit down, I lit a cigarette and began to pace the floor.

About ten minutes passed when the nurse came back out. She had Agent Jones' suit jacket and wallet in her hand. She came over and asked if she could talk to me. She said, "We need some information. What is his name?"

I told her, "His name is Franklin Jones, he lives in Atlanta." I pulled his driver's license out of his wallet and gave it to her. "You can use the driver's license for some of the information. I can tell you anything else you need to know."

She said, "You two are both dressed in black suits, what do you do anyway?"

I told her, "We are FBI agents."

She said, "I'm surprised to see a black FBI agent. I didn't know they existed." She continued, "When you first walked in here and told me your story, I thought you must be crazy. I didn't know that your friend was black."

I asked, "Is he going to be all right?"

She said, "That's a hard question to answer. The doctor is trying to stabilize him. He lost a lot of blood and his blood pressure is really low."

I said, "Do everything and anything you can for him."

I went back into the small waiting room. One minute I was sitting there thinking and the next someone was shaking me. I must have dozed off. It was a doctor.

He said, "My name is Doctor Bell. I've been working on your friend."

I asked, "How is he doing, Doctor Bell?"

He replied, "Well, we stabilized his blood pressure, but he lost a lot of blood. Also he still has the bullet lodged in his body. I don't have the equipment in this facility to help him anymore."

I said, "What are you saying, Doctor?"

He answered, "He needs to be taken to a facility that can help him more. I already phoned a hospital in Atlanta that will take him."

I put my head in my hands. I thought, *If he make it through all of what's he's already gone through it will be a miracle.*

The doctor put his hand on my shoulder and said, "I have an ambulance all ready to take him."

I said, "I'm going with him."

The doctor replied, "That won't be a problem."

We were on our way to Atlanta. I looked down at Agent Jones. He looked awful and was breathing very shallow. I gabbed his hand, it was still warm. I hoped he would hold on until we got to Atlanta. It would take about forty minutes. We were moving pretty fast. First thing I needed to do was call our field office and then his wife.

We finally arrived in Atlanta and started to drive through the city. I saw a huge six-story building come into view We went to the emergency entrance in the back. A bunch of nurses and a doctor came out. They took him down a long corridor. I walked in slowly looking around for a phone. A phone booth was located in the corner of the room.

I called our field office and told whoever was there what had happened. I really didn't know who I was speaking with. Everything seemed to be in a dreamlike state.

I had to call his wife. I sat there for a long time. *How am I going to tell her?* I was afraid of upsetting her. *I need to be tactful.*

I picked up the phone and dialed. It was about 12:30 at night. The phone rang for a long time. Finally, someone picked it up. It sounded like an older woman. I assumed it was his wife. She said, "Hello?" I couldn't speak. She said again, "Hello, who is this?"

I thought about what to say and finally said, "Mrs. Jones you don't know me, but my name is Agent Pierce. I've been working with your husband on a case."

She suddenly cut me short. "Agent Pierce, has something happened to my husband?"

I paused for a long time. I could hear her concern over the phone. I said, "Yes, Mrs. Jones, something has happened to your husband."

She started to cry. She said, "He's dead, isn't he?"

I began to talk to her again. "No, he's not dead. He's in the hospital. He's still alive, but he's been shot. I think you better get over here."

She tried to calm herself down. I told her which hospital we were at.

She said, "I know where it's at. I need to find someone to watch my children. I'll be right there as soon as I can." She hung up.

I asked one of the attendants who brought him in if I could see him. He said, "They are still working on him. He will be brought to this ward afterwards. You will be able to see him then. The ward is on the fifth floor."

I made my way to the elevator and went up to the fifth floor.

I walked down a long corridor to the end. On one side was a sign with an arrow pointing "Whites Only." The other sign had "Negroes Only." Even in a large city like Atlanta, there was no way of getting away from it. I headed down the corridor marked "Negroes Only."

When I did so, a white nurse grabbed my arm and stopped me. She said, "Sir, I think you want to go that way." She pointed towards the white person's ward.

I said, "No, ma'am, this is the way I want to go." She gave me a strange look and walked off in a huff.

There was an elderly nurse at the desk.

I asked her, "Have they brought up Franklin Jones yet?"

She said, "Please wait." She looked down at a chart and then said, "No."

I told her, "I'll wait."

I went over to a small seating area and sat down. I must have waited for about half an hour. Suddenly, a tall black woman came down the hall. I assumed she was Franklin's wife, so I rose to meet her. I put out my had to shake hers. Her hand was trembling very badly.

I said, "You must be Franklin's wife, Dorothy. I'm Agent Pierce, I spoke to you on the phone."

She replied, "Yes, I'm his wife. Do you know where he is?"

I told her, "He is still in surgery and hasn't come up yet."

We both sat down in the waiting room. We didn't speak. I thought it would be better if I didn't say anything.

After about a minute or so, she spoke. "Who shot him?"

I grabbed her hand and told her the whole story of what happened. She started to cry. She opened her purse and took a tissue out to wipe her eyes and nose. I tried to reassure her that everything would be all right, but I don't think she believed me.

She said, "I'm glad you were there. Who knows what might have happened to him."

I told her, "I'm just doing my job."

We sat there for about one hour and then I heard the elevator doors open. A couple of people dressed in white clothing came towards us pushing a gurney. We both got up. As it passed we saw that it was Franklin. She walked alongside them into the ward.

I was about to follow when the nurse behind the desk asked me, "Where are you going?"

I said, "I'm going in to see him."

She said, "Unless you're a family member, you're not allowed in there and by the looks of you, you're not family."

Her statement made me very angry. I pulled out my FBI badge and shoved it under her nose. I said, "Both he and I work for the FBI. That makes us family. Don't ever say something like that to me again."

I decided to sit down and wait. It was only right that his wife see him first.

When Franklin's wife came out, she walked over to me. She said, "He seems all right. They gave him something to make him sleep I'm going to stay here by his bed."

I asked her, "Are you going to be all right?"

She said, "I'll be fine. You need to go home and get some sleep."

I told her, "I'll do that, but I will be back here in the morning."

She smiled and hugged me. She whispered in my ear. "Thank you for being his partner. I don' know what would have happened to him if you weren't."

I smiled back. I told her goodbye and left the hospital.

I went back to the apartment that I was staying in while in Atlanta. I think I fell asleep around three in the morning.

When I awoke, the sun was shining in my face. It was about 6:00 A.M. I looked a mess. I was unshaven and had an unkempt look about me. My suit coat was one big wrinkle. I also needed a shower badly and took one. I dressed in the same suit and then made my way to the field office.

I went directly toward my office. As I walked, I got all kinds of looks. One person said to me. "You look like shit."

I got a cup of coffee and went into my office. I laid my arms down on the desk and folded them over. I put my head down on top of them. No sooner had I done this than someone knocked on my door. It was Julie, the office secretary.

She asked, "Are you all right?"

I looked up and said loudly, "No. Let me know when the field commander comes in." I got up, shut the door, and put my head back down.

A little while later I heard another knock on the door. It was Julie again. She said, "The boss is in."

I looked up and told her, "Thanks." I got up, tried to straighten out my suit, and walked to his office.

I walked in. "Good morning, Commander Holden."

He turned around and looked at me. He had a somewhat horrified look on his face. He said, "What in God's name happened to you last night?"

I started to tell him about the ambush and shooting. I told him, "Agent Jones was hit."

He fell back into his chair and asked, "How bad?"

I said, "He was shot in the stomach. Hopefully, he will pull through."

He asked, "Where is he?"

I told him, "He is at the Good Shepherd Hospital here in Atlanta."

He said, "Everyone here must go and visit him when he feels better." I was about to get up when he asked, "Where are you going?"

I said, "I'm going back down there. I needed to finish what I started."

He said, "I think you better not. I'm thinking of taking you off this case."

I asked, "Why? We were so close until this happened."

He said, "I don't think you're in the right frame of mind now."

I told him, "I'm all right. You have nothing to worry about. I need to finish this, if only for Agent Jones' sake."

I wanted to go back to Miner's Bluff to finish what I'd gone down there for—to find out who killed Nathaniel Johnson and put them away for the rest of their lives. I was going back with a vengeance and I was bringing a whole lot of help with me. FBI headquarters in Washington was sending at least twenty-five agents with me to help solve the crime once and for all.

Not only were they going to be charged with the murder of a young boy, but now they would also he charged with attempted murder of a government law enforcement officer. I was going to tear the town apart. No more playing by the rules. I had been given one week to get it over with and I would use any means possible to do it. I needed to wait a couple day before reinforcements arrived from Washington to Atlanta.

I went to visit Agent Jones several times while waiting for the other agents to come from Washington. He was always asleep when I did. The doctors were trying to keep him relaxed, so they had pumped him with pain medication and sedatives. He was looking a little better, but was still in great pain.

The day before I was to return to Miner's Bluff, I went to see him. He was finally awake when I entered his room. I stopped right inside the door. His wife was sitting on the other side of the bed, holding his hand. She looked at me and smiled. She started to get up.

As she did, she said to me, "I'll wait outside, you two have a lot to talk about."

I told her, "You don't have to go." But she insisted on leaving.

I walked over to his bedside. Franklin's head turned slowly around. I said, "You're looking better since the last time I saw you."

He replied, "You can tell me the truth. I look like shit, don't I?" He sort of did. He had so many tubes going into him and so many machines around him.

I put out my hand to shake his. He raised his arm very slowly. He still seemed to be very weak. I grabbed his hand quickly and held it.

I told him, "I'm going back down to Miner' Bluff. They gave me twenty-five men to go back with. We're not leaving until we have the people who did this to you in custody."

He smiled back and said, "You seem to be a man on a mission now."

I replied, "I guess I am and I'm probably going to get fired after everything is over."

Suddenly, he got a look on his face, so I asked, "What's wrong, what's the matter?"

He said, "Every so often, I get this shooting pain in my stomach. It usually passes very quickly." I must have had a horrified look on my face because he said, "Don't worry, the doctor said this was usual for what happened to me. I'm not going to die. I'm too pissed off to die."

I cracked a smile and so did he. I shook his hand and let go. I started to leave the room. He said, "Find the ones who did this."

I replied, "I won't come back until I do and I'm going to be praying for you."

He replied, "I'm going to pray for you too. You're going to need it more than me."

Outside his room I saw his wife coming down the hallway towards me. I said, "He seems a little better since I last saw him."

She said, "Yes, little by little, he's getting better. Still it's going to take a while before he's fully recovered."

I told her, "I'm going back to the town."

She seemed happy and afraid at the same time. She probably knew it was dangerous for me to go back. They had tried to kill us once. Since they failed, they would probably try again. I hugged her and left the hospital.

I was on my way back to the field office. Agent Jones was right. I was now on a mission. It went past the murder of a young child. What happened to me over the past three weeks had somehow changed me. It was no longer an investigation. It was a quest for justice. I was now fighting a way of life, a way of life that had been preserved for so many years by horrible acts of violence.

I arrived at the Atlanta field office and received instructions from my commanding officer. The men had arrived from Washington. All of them looked like they'd just graduate from high school. I brought them into a room to inform them where we were going and what to expect.

I said to them, "You will have to be on guard every minute you are there. It means nothing to them to just kill us. They already tried once."

I wanted to make sure that they weren't going down there naïve. I told them what I expected of them. Once I was finished, I told them, "Wait in the parking lot of the office."

I went to see my commander for the last time before I left. He told me, "Good luck and be careful."

I went down to the office parking lot. There were six black FBI cars sitting there. The men had driven them down from Washington. We started to load the cars up. There would be four to a car. We also loaded guns, rifles, and ammunition. If things went bad, we had to be prepared. I was going to get some answers and I was going to get them soon.

Everyone hopped into the cars and we made our way to the highway to Miner's Bluff. I would drive alone. It was about 10:00 A.M. I wanted to arrive early, so we would have most of the day to get things we needed done. It took about three-quarters of an hour to get to Miner's Bluff from Atlanta. The cars followed my lead, one black car after another.

Seven

We approached the town limits and as we drove in, people on the road just stopped and stared. We could tell by the expressions on their faces that something was up. My first stop was Sheriff Crawford's office. I had decided that we would use his office and jail. I was going to politely kick him out.

Before leaving Atlanta, I was able to get warrants to search and to take over anything and any place I wanted. I had the backing of the U.S. government and there was nothing they could do about it. If they tried, I could arrest them for obstruction of justice.

On the outskirts of town, I pulled over and stopped. The other agents followed. I got out and walked to the second car. I told the agents in each of the cars, "Be on the watch for anything suspicious and follow me into town."

I said, "We are heading straight to Sheriff Crawford's office, which is in the center of the town."

I parked in front of it. Some of the agents parked the cars next to me while the others parked on the opposite side of the street. The four agents in the second car came with me. I told the others, "Stay out here and be our guard."

The people who were on the street started to stop and stare.

I walked into Sheriff Crawford's office with the four agents behind me. I told them, "Keep your weapons ready just in case the sheriff wants to start something."

Dumb Deputy Hank was sitting behind his desk doing nothing as usual. I asked him, "Is Sheriff Crawford in?"

He said, "He is."

I told the agents, "Escort Deputy Hank outside for a few minutes."

The expression on his face was priceless as I kicked open the door to Sheriff Crawford's office.

He was sitting back in his chair reading a paper and smoking his rotten smelling cigars. He pulled down the paper and said, "Who the hell are you to barge right into my office?"

I took out my badge and I.D. I said, "I am a law officer for the United States government and this gives me the right." I then pulled out a warrant for his arrest. I told him, "I'm arresting you on conspiracy and tampering with evidence." He tried to voice his displeasure. I told him, "Shut up."

I told one of the agents, "Arrest him."

He grabbed Sheriff Crawford and turned him around. The agent started to put handcuffs on him. The sheriff started to plead with me. "I'll tell anything you want to know."

I asked, "I want to know who killed Nathaniel Johnson and who tried to kill me and my partner."

He said, "I don't know."

I said, "You're lying."

He said, "Honest, I don't know who killed him."

I said, "You're lying to me. You're the sheriff in this town. You know everything that goes on here."

He kept denying that he knew anything. I told the agent, "Put him in the jail cell. I will deal with him later."

I decided to go through the paperwork he had. I ordered some of the other agents, "Start cleaning out all the files and desk in the office. I want every shred of paper in there."

I left one agent to watch Sheriff Crawford. He would stay in jail until he told me what he knew. Deputy Hank stood outside of the office.

I told him, "For the time being you won't be working. Go home, but don't leave town." I thought about arresting Deputy Hank, but decided against it. He probably didn't know much about what was going on anyway.

We needed someplace to stay and I wanted to stay as close to the center of town as possible. Before Deputy Hank left, I asked him, "Is there anywhere to stay in town?"

He pointed across the street to three-story building. He said, "It's a boarding house and you can find some rooms in there."

I walked across the street, taking a couple agents with me. The others stayed in their cars. I entered the boarding house and there was a sign on the wall that said: "Rooms to Rent." I walked over to the counter where a middle-aged man stood.

He asked, "Can I help you?"

I said, "I need to rent a couple of rooms."

He asked, "How many?"

I said, "Probably about ten of them."

He looked at me with a surprised look on his face. He said, "I have to check to see if I have that many available."

He walked into a back room and then came back out. He said, "I only have eight rooms."

I said, "I'll take them."

He said, "It will be fifteen dollars a week for each room."

I told him, "I'll pay for a week up front."

I told the agents, "Go out and tell the other agents where they will be staying and to come over."

There were about twenty of them in the building's lobby. I told them, "Get your stuff out of the cars and bring it here." I handed out seven keys to different agents and told them, "You might have to stay three to four in a room. I'll let you decide who stays with whom. I'm keeping one room for myself."

While the others agents brought their stuff in, I walked over to the jail. I had three of the agents there. I spoke to one. "How is Sheriff Crawford doing?"

He replied, "Not so good, sir. He's been complaining ever since you left." I smiled.

I walked back to Sheriff Crawford's cell. He said to me, "You can't do this to me. I got my rights."

I thought it was funny coming from him. How many so-called rights had he trampled on while he was sheriff? How many blacks got railroaded while he turned a blind eye? I said to him, "I'll allow you one phone call. Maybe you should call your lawyer, because you're going to need one after I get through with you."

He replied, "You're at least gonna to feed me, aren't you?"

I told him, "I'll think about it." Luckily, he wasn't married and probably had no home life. No one in particular would miss him.

I told two of the agents, "Go over to the boarding house." I left one at the jail to guard the sheriff. I decided I would rotate different people to watch him. I needed as many agents as possible. I might have to arrest half the people in town and wanted to be sure I wasn't caught undermanned. I told the agent, "If you need me, I'll be at the boarding house. Call me on the phone if you need anything."

I went back to my car first and got my briefcase. In it was all the evidence I had obtained so far on the case, which was-

116

n't much, mostly circumstantial—a few photos, some paperwork and a few odds and ends. No hard evidence, no smoking gun. It was going to be hard to get a conviction from it. I needed more. Hopefully, by the end of the week, I would have it.

My main plan was to make life miserable for the three suspects—Pernel Williams, Joseph Fuller, and Andrew Whittaker. I had already spoken to two of them. I had yet to speak to Andrew Whittaker. I'd tried earlier when Agent Jones was with me, but he hadn't wanted to speak to us at the time. Let's just say he let his gun speak for him.

I decided to have them tailed from the time they got up in the morning until the time they went to bed. Wherever they went, I would have them followed. They wouldn't be able to make a move without one of my fellow agents knowing about it. I hoped it would make one of them crack. All I needed was one confession, just one to spill their guts.

Two days passed since putting my plan into action. I had decided to work out of the sheriff's office. Sheriff Crawford was still in jail. I thought of letting him out, but was afraid he might skip town. If someone did crack and started talking, I wanted Sheriff Crawford to be close by. I thought they might implicate the sheriff and I wanted him right where I could see him.

I was sitting at Sheriff Crawford's desk when suddenly, I heard a commotion outside the office. I walked out to see what was happening. It was Pernel Williams. He was asking for Sheriff Crawford.

I told Mr. Williams, "The sheriff is indisposed at the moment, Can I help you?"

He started yelling very loudly at me. "I want you to call off your men."

I said, "Whatever do you mean?"

He replied, "You know what I'm talking about. I see them sitting outside my house all the time and following me wherever I go."

I said to Mr. Williams, "Look, Mr. Williams, they're only looking out for you, making sure nothing happens to you. Anyway, if you're not doing anything wrong, they're not going to bother you."

He replied, "I have my rights, you can't come down here and do whatever you want. I'm going to get a lawyer and sue you."

I said, "Go right ahead, do whatever you want, but until something stops me from doing what I'm doing, I'm going to continue to do it."

He got up and walked out in a huff.

It looked as if it was getting to him and I thought he might be the first to crack. Still, I wasn't just going to wait for that to happen. I needed to go out and do more investigating to gather evidence, however little it might be. I thought my next move would be to talk to Andrew Whittaker. I decided to take a nice-sized force with me, just in case he decided to make trouble.

I went over to the boarding house. I went and knocked on a couple doors. The first room had three men in it. I told them, "Come with me."

We walked down to the lobby of the boarding house. I explained the situation to them. I took three in my car and the rest followed in another car.

We drove to Andrew Whittaker's house and I parked in front of the house. I told the other car, "Pull up farther and park down the road, just in case he decides to try and sneak out."

The two agents who were watching him were still parked outside his home. I told them, "Wait in your car. I'm going to send you back and have another two watch him after I talk to him."

It was about 10:00 A.M. I hoped he was there. I walked up to the front door with three agents backing me up, just in case. I wasn't taking any chances. I pounded on the door, but no one came. I pounded it again. I saw thorough the screen someone coming towards the door. It was Andrew Whittaker and he wasn't happy.

He asked, "What the hell do you want?"

I told him, "I need to ask you some questions."

He replied, "You tried to ask me questions before. I thought I made my answer quite clear."

I said, "Oh, I hope you're not thinking of pulling a gun on me again, because if you do, you'll be dead before you can get your hand on it."

He said, "Is that a threat?"

I said, "No, that's a promise and fact. Now, if you could step out here for a few minutes, I'd like to ask you a question or two."

He came out the door. He said, "Let's walk down to the street. I don't want my family hearing none of this."

I began to question him about the murder of Nathaniel Johnson. Of course, he knew nothing about it and had nothing to do with it. I told him, "I have evidence and witnesses placing you at the scene of the crime."

He just laughed and said, "You can't prove nothing anyway."

I said, "I can prove a lot of things. Don't be so sure of yourself, Mr. Whittaker."

Suddenly, I heard a small voice yell out the door. It was a young girl, who looked about ten. I couldn't really see her face. She looked like she might have had blonde hair. She asked, "What's the matter, Daddy?"

Andrew Whittaker turned towards the door and yelled

back, "Nothing, sweetie, these nice men are asking Daddy about something. Why don't you go back and watch TV."

He turned to me and said, "Do you enjoy doing what you're doing?"

I asked him, "What do you mean?"

He said, "I mean coming over to my home and scaring my daughter."

I said, "We only came over here to ask some questions, that's all."

He replied, "Well, I'm finished answering your questions from now on. If you ever come over here again, I might have to protect myself."

I just shook my head and laughed. I said, "You do what you have to do, but if I have a question and the answer's over here, I'm coming to get it."

I started to walk back to my car. Mr. Whittaker said something to me, but I didn't hear what. I asked him, "Repeat what you just said."

He came down closer to me and spoke, "I said, why do you care about some little nigger boy that was killed? You don't live here. Why does it concern you?"

I replied, "The first reason is, it's my job, but the most important is because somebody has to care and apparently no one else but me down here does."

He didn't say anything else and walked back to his house. I walked to my car. I would probably be coming back in the near future.

I went back to the sheriff's office. I needed to make some calls. First one was about Pernel Williams's car. Supposedly it had been stolen, but no police report was ever made.

I thought *You need a police report for insurance purposes.* I needed to find out if an insurance company ever paid out on the stolen car. If one had, that meant a lot of people had lied to me, including the sheriff. Even if I could prove it, it still was going to be hard to connect everyone with the murder.

I parked in front of the sheriff's office. I only saw a few agents around the town, so most must till be in the boarding house. They were getting bored as there seemed to be nothing for them to do. They didn't understand why I needed them, but hopefully in a few days they would.

I walked into the sheriff's office. As usual, Sheriff Crawford was complaining loudly. He'd been locked up for the last three days. I decided to let him go, but I would have him tailed.

I said to him, "Good news today, Sheriff. I'm letting you go."

He said, "Oh, that's real kind of you to do this. What, you couldn't find anything on me?"

I told one of the agents, "Unlock the jail door."

Sheriff Crawford gathered up his things and walked out of the cell.

As he started toward the door, he turned around and said, "You think you're real smart. You're in big trouble. You're going to pay for what you done to me."

I looked at him with a smile while gazing at the other agents in the office. I said, "Did you hear that, gentlemen? I think he threatened me. I think that's a federal offense, isn't it?"

His demeanor suddenly changed. I wasn't going to throw him back in jail. I just wanted to scare him a little. I said, "Don't worry, you can leave. You stink up this place, anyway."

I got into my car. I needed to go over to see Reverend Jackson and his wife. I'd been so busy that I hadn't visited them yet. I wanted to make sure everything was all right with them. I looked down at the passenger seat. There was a small piece of paper lying there all folded up. I picked it up and unfolded it. It contained a short message. I read it:

If you want to know who killed that little boy, you need to search Jimmy Dugan's house.

I thought, *Who is Jimmy Dugan? And how does he fit into all of this?*

I went back into the office. I needed to know where Jimmy Dugan lived, so I checked the phone book. There was only one James Dugan. I assumed he was the Jimmy Dugan I needed to speak with. He lived at 105 Summit Road. I called the field office. I needed a search warrant to search his house. I wondered what I would find there. I would have to wait until another day to find out.

I went back out to the car. I still wanted to visit Reverend Jackson and his wife. I drove to their home. I knocked on their door. I saw someone coming towards the door. It was Mrs. Jackson. She threw open the door and gave me big hug.

She told me, "Come in."

I asked, "How are you doing?"

She said, "Oh, Otis and I are doing all right. A little trouble now and then. How is Franklin doing?"

I said, "Franklin's doing better now. He's still in the hospital in Atlanta. I didn't think he was going to make it, but he's getting better."

She said, "Otis and I have to visit him. What hospital is he in?"

I wrote down the hospital and address for her. I asked her, "Where's Reverend Jackson at?"

She said, "Oh he's at the church preparing for Sunday service. Maybe you can come to the service."

I said, "Yes, I think I would like that."

As I got up to leave, Mrs. Jackson said to me, "Going so soon? I thought maybe you could stay for lunch."

I said, "I have to get back. I'm still working on the case."

She seemed sad I was leaving. I guess she missed Franklin and me. I gave her a hug and told her, "I'll be seeing you and Mr. Jackson later."

I walked to my car. Mrs. Jackson stood on the porch as I drove away and waved as I went by. Little did she know that I was watching out for her and her husband. Agents had been staying outside her home since I'd been back. I didn't want to tell them because I thought it might frighten her. She probably would have not wanted them there anyway. She was a proud woman.

I went straight to my room at the boarding house and started to look at the evidence I had. I must have looked at the stuff a hundred times. I looked at the note again. *Who is this Jimmy Dugan? What will I find at his home? There's no murder weapon, like a gun or knife. What could it be?*

I'd have to wait until tomorrow anyway to find out. I needed to get some sleep. I put everything back into the briefcase and went to bed.

About 8:00 A.M. there was a knock on my door. It was the agent who had been at the sheriff's office all night. He had a piece of paper in his hand. He said, "Sir, one of our fellow agents dropped this off. I thought it was very important."

I grabbed it from his hand and looked at it. It was the search warrant I needed. I thanked him and sent him on his way. I had what I needed now.

I took my shower and quickly dressed. I went and knocked on one of the other doors. I told the agents inside, "Get dressed. We're going out on a mission."

They seemed excited. A lot of them had just been sitting

around with nothing to do. It would be their first bit of action.

I drove over to Jimmy Dugan's house along with four agents just in case I had any trouble. As was so often the case, the neighborhood that the people lived in was not particularly nice. There were a lot of run-down homes. Most of the roads were not paved. As you drove them, a lot of dirt kicked up that eventually made its way into the car and your mouth.

I started looking for the house. There were no numbers that were apparent, so I had to stop and get out of the car to look for an address. I walked down the road a little, looking for the right number. Finally, I came to the house. It looked like the others I had visited, old and needing a paint job. I walked up to the front door. Two agents followed me and the other two waited in the street near the car.

I knocked on the door. A young woman, who looked barely eighteen, answered the door.

I asked her, "Is Jimmy Dugan home?"

She said, "No, he's not here right now."

I replied, "Miss, I really need to talk to him."

She asked, "Who are you?"

I told her, "I am from the FBI and I am investigating a crime."

She asked, "Would you like to come in?"

I told the other agents to wait outside and then went inside. I didn't want to frighten her since she might be able to tell me thing I needed to know.

I heard a baby crying in the distance. She told me, "Sit down on the couch and wait a minute."

I had to remove a few things before I could sit. She came back holding the baby on her left side. She sat down on the chair next to me and fed the baby a bottle.

I started to ask her some questions. "How do you know Jimmy Dugan?"

She replied, "He's my husband and the baby's father."

I said, "You look too young to be married and have a baby."

She said, "I'm nineteen, I don't think that's young." She continued to feed the baby.

I was about to ask her another question, when she said something that shocked me. "You got the note didn't you?"

I was stunned. I said, "What did you say?"

She repeated, "I said, you got the note I left for you in your car."

I said, "You left the note in the car. Why?"

She didn't answer. She took the bottle out of the baby's mouth, got up, and took the baby back into the bedroom. She came out and sat across from me again.

I asked her, "Why did you put the note in my car?"

She got up and walked to the window. She looked out of it, peering left to right. She came back down and sat next to me. She said, "If Jimmy ever found out I talked to you, he'd kill me right where I'm standing."

She was starting to try my patience. She knew something and I wanted to know what it was. I pressed her again.

She said, "You can't prove that I put that note into your car." She started to tell her story. "I know you been going around town trying to find out about that little black boy that was killed. You been asking a lot of questions about certain people. They ain't exactly happy about it. If you ask me who did it, I couldn't tell you and wouldn't. If you need to search the house, I'm not going to stop you."

I thought, *Is this woman crazy? What the hell is she talking about? It seems that if I came here for a straight answer, I'm not going to get it.* I asked, "So what you're saying to me, if I search the house, I'll find out who killed that young boy, right?"

She just stared at me without answering. She grabbed my arm to pull me up and said, "You better hurry, Jimmy will be home in about an hour. I don't want him to find you here. There will be hell to pay for me if he does."

I went to the front door and called the other two agents in from the front porch. I told one, "Search the bedroom. Check everywhere, in drawers, in closets, under the mattress."

The agents checked the other bedroom while I checked the living area and kitchen. I pulled out drawers and checked under everything. I must have torn up the house for about half an hour. I didn't find much. The other agents came out of the bedrooms every once in a while to show me things. None were important to the case. I started to wonder why she called us. I wasn't too happy about it.

I called the other agents back into the living room. I said, "I think we wasted enough time doing this."

Jimmy Dugan's wife was on the porch smoking a cigarette.

I said to her, "Come back in."

She said, "Did you find anything yet?"

I said, "No, not yet." I was about to leave, when I asked her, "Do you have a basement?" I hadn't thought of it until then.

She said, "No." I waved to the other agents and walked to the door. Suddenly, she said, "We have a crawl space."

I asked her, "Where?"

She pointed towards the ceiling between the living room and kitchen.

I walked over to it. A large square had been cut out of the ceiling. It looked like a piece of wood was covering it. I found a broom in the kitchen; I took the end and pushed the piece of wood up and out of the way.

I asked her, "Do you have a flashlight handy?"

She went and checked in the kitchen, but couldn't find one.

I told one of the agents, "Go out to the car. I have one in the glovebox."

The agent came back in with it. I told the two agents, "Boost me up."

I pulled myself up and into the crawl space. I turned on the flashlight. I shined it back and forth to see in front of me. It was very small and tight. I crawled along a joist. I scanned the light from one side to the other. It was dusty and hot. The dust kept getting in my mouth and eyes. When I shined the flashlight down to the end of the crawl space, something caught my eye. I had to maneuver very carefully as I was afraid that I would fall through the ceiling.

I made it to the end of the crawl space. I found what looked like a large box. I put it in an upright position and pulled it towards me. Luckily the box wasn't locked so I opened it. I aimed the flashlight inside the box. The first thing I saw looked like a camera. I pulled it out and looked at it. It looked like a plain old camera to me.

What does this have to do with the murder? What's so important about this?

Right next to it, I noticed a book. I picked it up and put it on my lap. I held the flashlight under my chin. I aimed the light at the book and opened it.

What I saw stunned me. There were pictures in it that looked like crime scenes. Pictures of dead bodies. Most were lying on the ground. Some of the others were hanging from the trees. I didn't understand it. I put everything back into the box and pushed it down the crawl space to the opening.

I called one of the agents, "Come and grab it."

He pulled over a chair to stand on. He then grabbed it and put it on the ground. I made my way out of the crawl space to the floor below.

I told Mrs. Dugan, "I'm confiscating the box as evidence." She said nothing and turned away. I told one of the agents, "Put the box in my car."

I told her, "I'm leaving now, but I will be coming back."

She seemed very upset. She might have betrayed her husband and I wanted to know why. *Why did she do this? I might have to wait for my answer for some time.*

Eight

I returned to my room at the boarding house. The box was sitting in front of me. I opened it and took the book out again. I wanted to see the pictures in better light. I started going through the pictures again. They were so horrible and cruel it was hard to look at them.

I thought, *Why would anyone want to take these pictures and keep them? The person who did this is a pretty sick person.* I went through all the pictures. *What's the point of this book?*

I was about to put everything back into the box when I looked down. I piece of brown paper had been put on the bottom of the box. It looked like it didn't belong there. I grabbed it and lifted it up. Under it was a large manila envelope. I pulled the envelope out and opened it. There were two large pictures in it. I pulled them out.

I was both shocked and excited at the same time. One of the pictures was of a small boy hanging from a tree. I couldn't make out the face, but I could tell by the body's length it was Nathaniel Johnson. It had been taken sometime at night. The other was exactly like the first one, except for one thing—it was taken with a large view. I could make out every one of the faces—Pernel Williams, Joseph Fuller and Andrew Whittaker. Jimmy Dugan probably took the pictures.

I went into my briefcase and got out the pictures Sheriff Crawford had turned over to me. One of them was of Nathaniel Johnson taken the next day during the daylight while he was still hanging from the tree. I put the pictures side by side. There was no denying it. The person who took the picture for the sheriff's department and the one who took the picture at night were one in the same—the fourth person. I finally had it. I finally had the big break in the case I needed. A simple picture would do them in.

I finally had the bastards. There would be no denying it now. The only problem was who actually killed Nathaniel Johnson. Was it just one or all of them? I decided to arrest all of them. I had probable cause and also evidence to use against them. I'd arrest them and try to wring a confession out of one. It was my turn to play mind games with them.

Our first stop was Pernel Williams' house. I took four carloads of agents with me. I thought it might get ugly if he resisted arrest. I banged on the door loudly and waited for about ten seconds. I banged again and yelled into the house, "Come out with your hands up."

I swung the door wide open with my gun drawn. He came into the living room with a stunned look on his face.

I told him, "Turn around and put your hands behind your back." I told one of the agents, "Cuff him." I said to Pernel, "I'm arresting you for the murder of Nathaniel Johnson."

He turned around to me and said, "You got to be joking. You can't arrest me. You ain't got no proof."

I told him, "I have all the proof I need."

While the agents took him out to the car, he kept saying, "You're going to pay for this."

Our next stop was Joseph Fuller. I knew he had young children, so I decided to go up to the house alone and kept the other agents in the cars. I knocked on the door. His girlfriend came to the door.

I asked, "Is your boyfriend home?"

She said, "He's at work."

130

I asked her, "Where?"

She said, "He works at a gas station."

She gave me directions and we went there.

He was pumping gas when we drove up. I could tell by the look on his face that he knew something was up.

I told him, "You are under arrest for murder."

He didn't resist at all and put his hands behind his back. As we led him to he car, he said, "I knew this day would come. I just didn't know when."

We had two in custody and still two to go. Jimmy Dugan would be last. I was going after Andrew Whittaker first. I had a feeling he wasn't going without a fight. I had Pernel Williams and Joseph Fuller each sitting in one of the cars. Two agents sat on each side of them with their guns drawn, just in case either tried anything.

We made our way to Andrew Whittaker's house. We didn't know how he would act. He was like dynamite, ready to explode at any minute. I hoped that he would come easy and that he wouldn't resist. I didn't want any more bloodshed. I needed to be tactful. I didn't want to give him any reason to start shooting. I didn't want innocent people to get hurt or even killed.

I was just outside the yard to his house. Thankfully, the dog was not in the yard. We would have an easier time now. Nothing would give our presence away. I walked up to his door with two other agents, one on my right side and the other on my left side. I wanted them hidden from view with their guns drawn and facing the door. I had the other agents crouch behind the cars with their guns drawn just in case.

I pounded on the door. No one answered. I thought, *Maybe he's not here. Maybe he found out about us coming and left town.* I pounded again. Finally I saw a male figure making his way to the door. It looked like Andrew Whittaker.

He came right to the front door, but did not come out.

We were face to face through the screen of the door. I told him, "Andrew Whittaker, I'm placing you under arrest for the murder of Nathaniel Johnson."

He started laughing. "You got to be kidding me."

I told him, "Come out with your hands up in the air."

He laughed again and said, "I'm not going anywhere with you. I'm going back to watch some TV."

I said, "If you don't come out, I'm going to come in and get you."

He said, "Go ahead and try."

There was only one way he would come with us and that was to be forcefully dragged out of his house. I drew my gun out and swung open the door. I told him, "Put your hands up."

He turned around and laughed at me again. He said, "Why don't you shoot me? You won't because you don't have the guts."

I told him again, "Put your hands behind your back."

He refused again and said, "I dare you to try and handcuff me. If you do, one of us is going to die and it's not going to be me."

I'd had enough. I lunged towards him and tried to grab him by the arm. When I did, he took swing at me and we started to scuffle. We began wrestling with each other. Suddenly, he tried to reach for my gun. I yelled outside for the other agents, who rushed with their guns drawn and aimed at Andrew Whittaker.

One of them told Mr. Whittaker, "Stop or we will shoot."

I had a sick feeling that Andrew Whittaker would rather be shot than go with me. Both agents put their guns back into their holsters and tried to grab any part of Andrew Whittaker's body they could.

All four of us crashed onto the floor into a heap. The other agents were able to get Andrew Whittaker's arms behind his body and I put the cuffs on him. He continued to struggle while I did so, kicking and screaming and cursing at me. The agents pulled him off the floor. He fought them the whole time in an attempt to get away. He tried to kick me as well.

I told him, "You could have come with us peacefully, but you decided not to."

The agents started towards the door. As they walked by me, Mr. Whittaker tried to spit in my face. Luckily, he missed. He fought and screamed the whole time the agents dragged him to the car, making threats to me. They threw him into the car.

I told them, "Go back to the sheriff's office and put him in a jail cell. I'm going to check the house out."

I searched all around in the house, but found nothing of importance.

It was time to pick up Jimmy Dugan. I drove to his house with two agents in tow. I had been there only a few hours earlier and was hopeful he would be home. After his arrest, we would have all the characters in the sick plot.

I knocked on the door. I could hear a voice coming from inside. It was a man's voice. I heard him say, "Don't worry, I'll get it, Beth." He came to the door.

I said, "Are you Jimmy Dugan?"

He said, "Who wants to know?"

I replied, "Mr. Dugan, my name is Agent Pierce. I'm with the FBI and I'm here to arrest you for the murder of Nathaniel Johnson."

He said, "Who is he? I never heard of him."

I said, "I don't have time for a discussion."

I proceeded to open the front door. I told him, "Put your hands behind your back."

His wife came back into the room. She was crying. He

turned to her and asked, "Beth, honey, what's going on?" She didn't answer.

I told him again, "Put your hands behind your back." I motioned the two agents to put him into handcuffs.

He kept repeating, "I didn't do nothing. I swear I didn't do nothing."

He didn't give us any trouble. I looked at his wife, who was still crying. I told her, "That was a hard thing that you did, but it was the right thing to do."

She said, "Just get out of my house and leave me alone."

We left and went back to the sheriff's office.

I walked into the sheriff's office. I heard all them saying how they were innocent and complaining about their rights. I decided to keep them away from one another. There were seven jail cells, so I wasn't going to let them even look at each other while they were there. Soon the interrogations would begin. I was going to play mind games with them. I was going to pit one against another. Hopefully one would crack and spill his guts on all the others.

I was ready to start the interrogation when the front door of the sheriff's office flew open. It was Sheriff Crawford. He shouted at me, "What the hell are you doing? Going around arresting all these people. Accusing them of murder."

I told him, "I have sufficient evidence linking the four to the murder."

He said, "You have gone off the deep end, boy. These gentlemen didn't have anything to do with that. I had already investigated this. I told you before, it was the Ku Klux Klan. You went and arrested innocent men."

I got up and walked over to Sheriff Crawford. I'd had enough of the windbag. I got right into his face and said to him, "If you don't shut that mouth of yours up, I'm going to tape it shut." I called over who of the agent. They stood on each side of him I spoke to Sheriff Crawford again. "I'm placing you under arrest."

He shouted back, "For what?"

I replied, "For tampering with evidence and for accessory to murder."

He started to laugh. "You're never going to make them charges stick."

I told the agents, "Take him back to one of the jail cells."

I decided to interrogate Joseph Fuller first. I thought he would be more likely to break. He didn't seem as mean-spirited as Pernel Williams or Andrew Whittaker, who both seemed to have a stronger constitution. I was betting my money that Joseph would tell me everything.

I had an agent bring Joseph Fuller to one of the back rooms of the jail. As they passed Whittaker's cell I heard him yell at Fuller, "You better not talk, Fuller. You better stick to our story or else. 'Cause if you don't, once I get out here you're dead."

Once he was in the back room with me, I had one of the agents stand outside the room just in case. The room had a table and two chairs. I sat down on one side of the table and asked Joseph Fuller to sit on the other.

He hesitated at first, so I asked him again, "Please sit down, because truthfully you're not getting out of here until we talk."

Finally he sat down. I turned on the tape recorder that was next to my left arm and I started questioning him. "What's your name and where do you live?"

He answered truthfully.

I told him, "The next questions I am going to ask I want you tell me the truth. Mr. Fuller, you're in a lot of trouble. I have sufficient evidence that places you at the scene of the crime. You're facing murder charges. This is a federal offense."

He just stared at me without any expression.

I said, "Let's make this easier on yourself. I know you didn't murder that young boy. I think you know who did. Just tell me everything you know and maybe we can work something out."

He said, "I don't know anything. I told you before when you asked me."

I said, "Fine, so this is how it's going to be." I got up and walked to the door. I told the agent outside the door, "Go get the photos for me."

I sat back down in the chair and was about to continue my questioning when the agent brought the photos in.

I asked him again, "Tell me all you know. If you had nothing to do with it, then there is no problem for you to tell me about it."

He resisted again. He insisted that he hadn't been there and didn't know anything about it.

I decided it was time to use my ace card. I started to pull the photo out of the manila envelope. Joseph Fuller got a strange look on his face. I turned the one with just Nathaniel Johnson hanging in the tree on the table and pushed it towards him.

I said, "Do you recognize this person in the photo?"

He said, "I never seen that boy before." He pushed the photo back towards me. "Is that supposed to impress me, 'cause it doesn't."

I took the second photos with all three of them in it and pushed it towards him. His angry face turned to shock. He picked it up.

I said to him, "Do you recognize anybody in this photo?"

He just sat there stunned, but didn't say anything. Finally he put the photo back down and said, "I'm not saying anything until I see a lawyer. Isn't that the law?"

136

I said, "Fine, when you get hold of your lawyer, we can talk again." I walked to the door and told the agent, "Take him back and bring me Jimmy Dugan."

Jimmy Dugan was brought in the room. He seemed the nervous type, always fidgety. I could tell he was really nervous. I asked him the same questions I asked Joseph Fuller and pretty much got the same answers. I pulled out the photo of the three, Joseph Fuller, Pernel Williams and Andrew Whittaker. I showed it to him. He looked at it. I could tell by the look on his face that he knew it was his photo.

I asked him, "Do you recognize those people in that photo?"

I saw he was perspiring. He looked at me and said, "You know who they are as well as I do." He was trying to tell me who they were without incriminating himself.

I said, "Yes, I do, I see three, but I don't see the one who shot this picture. Now who could it be?"

He replied, "You know who took the photo. Why are you playing this game?"

I said, "What game? I'm jut trying to get information. That's my job."

He leaned back into his chair and folded his arms across his chest. He said, "I'm not saying anymore until I see a lawyer."

I got up from the table and told one of the agents, "Take him back to the jail cell."

This is great, I thought. *I'm getting to them.*

I needed one to crack and to do it soon. I was afraid if it went on too long, they would be able to get out of jail and disappear, maybe never to be found. Time was not on my side.

Next was Pernel Williams. I had interviewed him twice before and had never got very much information out of him. *What will he do now knowing that there are three others being charged with him? Will he be willing to say more now?* I had to take my chances.

I asked one of the agents, "Go back and get Pernel Williams and bring him to me."

He came into the room and sat down. He leaned into the chair and folded his arms across his chest. He started to talk. "I don't know what that pipsqueak Jimmy Dugan told you, but I'm not saying nothing."

I replied, "He told me a lot of things. I guess you don't want to hear what he told me then."

He gave me a look like he didn't care. I wasn't going to tell him exactly what Jimmy Dugan said to me. I thought if he thought Jimmy Dugan ratted on him, he would tell me what happened that night.

I said to him, "Jimmy told me everything. How you three dragged that little boy into the car. How you killed him and hung him in that tree. How you tried to burn the car so no one would find it." The last bit of information seemed to pique his interest. I said, "Oh, you didn't know we found your stolen car, did you?"

He had a shocked look on his face. I continued telling him about it. "I found your car in a park near Healy's Lake. It seems someone tried to torch it. I know it belongs to you because I have the vehicle identification number off the car and it matched the one that belonged to you at one time."

Pernel Williams was no longer leaning back in the chair with his arms folded. His arms were on the table and he kept rubbing them together. He seemed nervous.

I needed to keep him nervous and off guard, so I told him, "I hate to tell you Jimmy Dugan, Andrew Whittaker, and Joseph Fuller have told me they are willing to sign a full confession that you killed Nathaniel Johnson."

Pernel Williams replied, "You're lying, they would never do that."

I said, "But they did. If you think they're going to take the rap for you, you're mistaken."

I called the agents in to take Pernel back to the jail cell. I got up and said to him, "I have all the information and evidence I need to bring this to trial. I decided to hold you for murder and I am letting Jimmy Dugan, Joseph Fuller, and Andrew Whittaker go."

I saw he was really getting nervous and was sweating bullets. I told the agent, "Take him back."

The agent grabbed his arm and started to escort him out the door when suddenly, Pernel Williams said, "Wait a minute." He stood silently for a few seconds, then came back into the room and sat down. He said, "I'll tell you everything you want to know."

I thought, *Great. My bluff worked. I was hoping he would do this.*

I told him, "I will only listen to you if you are willing to sign a confession and be willing to testify against whoever killed Nathaniel Johnson."

He said, "Yes, I'll do whatever you want. I'm not going to take the rap for something I didn't do."

I had the tape recorder sitting next to me. I told him, "I am going to record everything you tell me." I got a piece of paper and typed on it: "Confession by Pernel Williams" and dated it. I made him sign it. I would type in the confession later.

I told him, "Start from the beginning."

He started his story. "It all started when that nigger boy made a pass at this little white girl. We were all over at Andrew Whittaker's house. Andrew Whittaker was really pissed off about it. He decided we should teach that boy a lesson. We had been drinking that night and we were all a little drunk. Well, we all hopped into my car and went looking for

him. Andrew knew where he lived, so we drove over there."
He stopped suddenly.

I asked, "Why are you stopping?"

He said, "My mouth is dry. I need something to drink."

I got up from the table and got some water. He took a
big sip of it. I told him, "Continue."

He started to talk again. "Well, we saw him walking
down the road. We drove a little, passed him, and stopped
up ahead. As he was passing the car, we grabbed and
dragged him in the car. He was kicking and swinging his
arms like mad. I got in the back and held his feet. Joseph got
in the front with Jimmy. Andrew started to beat the kid. I
told him to stop, but he didn't. He seemed to stop moving. I
could see blood coming out of his nose. Andrew told Jimmy
to drive to the woods outside of town. He did. He told Jimmy
to pull off to the side of the road. Andrew got out of the car.
He started to drag the boy by his one arm into the woods. I
really didn't know if the boy was still alive."

He stopped again and took another drink of water, then
he continued with his story. "He dragged him into the woods
and then let him drop to the ground. He started kicking and
stomping on him. I ran over and tried to stop him. This was-
n't the plan; we were just going to scare him. I asked Andrew
why he did this. He said, 'I need to teach him a lesson in
manners.' He told me, Joseph and Jimmy went to get some
wood for a bonfire. We gathered some wood. He told me to
get the gasoline and rope I had in the car and bring it back.
We put the wood in a pile and I poured some gasoline on it
and lit it. Andrew then took the rope and made a noose and
put it around the boy's neck. He then took the other end and
threw it over the tree limb. He climbed up the tree and
started to pull the rope up. He pulled it until the boy was
about seven or eight feet off the ground."

140

I decided to stop the tape recorder. He asked, "Why are we stopping?"

I said, "I need a drink of water now." I poured myself a glass of water and sat back down at the table. I told him, "Continue."

"He was just hanging there. I think he was probably dead before he was hung. Andrew told Jimmy to go and get his camera. He wanted a picture of this as a souvenir. Jimmy left and came back with his camera. He took one picture first and then another. They're the ones you have. It was all Andrew Whittaker's idea. He beat the boy, he hung him, and he killed him. Neither Jimmy or Joseph or me had anything to do with his murder."

Pernel Williams stopped talking and leaned back in his chair. I said to him, "I'm glad you told me this. I'm glad you told me the truth. You, Jimmy, and Joseph are still going to face charges of accessory, but not murder charges. If you cooperate and testify in court, I might be able to get you immunity, but that's only if you are willing to testify that Andrew Whittaker committed the crime. If you refuse or if you back out once you said you would, I'll nail your ass to the wall."

I told the agent, "Take him back to his jail cell. I will deal with him and the others tomorrow."

I decided not to talk to Andrew Whittaker. It wouldn't help anyway. I knew he wouldn't talk, even if I had all the evidence in the world that showed he did it. He was never ever going to confess. I needed one of his buddies to do that. Anyway, I already knew he was the murderer. I just needed someone other than myself to say he was. I'd found that person in Pernel Williams.

I couldn't let on that I knew who did it and why. I knew I had to keep them pitted against each other. I wanted to let them believe that one told on the other. I was bluffing and hoped it would work. I decided to talk to Andrew Whittaker the next day. I thought I'd let him stew for a little bit. He was going to be in for a big surprise.

It was early the next morning when I decided to bring Andrew Whittaker in and talk to him. I thought it was going to be fun. I told the two agents to bring him to the room. Of course, he wasn't going to come nicely and fought the agents the whole time. I knew I wasn't going to get a confession out of him. I just wanted to see how he reacted when I told him that all his friends had decided to rat on him.

The agent had to drag him into the room. They held him by his arms.

He said, "Will you tell your goons to let go of me?"

I told the agents, "Let him go." I said to him, "Sit down."

He said, "I'm not sitting down, 'cause I'm not telling you anything."

I replied, "I rather you sit down yourself, but if I have to, I will make you sit down with the help of my agents." He stood there like a statute, not moving a muscle. I said, "Well, I guess we'll have to do it the hard way."

I nodded my head to the agents. I kicked out the chair with my foot and the agent slammed Andrew Whittaker down in the chair.

I decided to keep the two agents in the room, one on each side of Mr. Whittaker. I also made them handcuff Andrew Whittaker to the chair.

I started telling him what I had. I said, "Mr. Whittaker, I have information and evidence that points to you as the murderer of Nathaniel Johnson."

Before I could continue, he interrupted me. He said, "You don't have shit on me. You know why, because I didn't do anything."

I told him, "But I do." I began to tell him everything. "I

have people who can identify you at the scene of the crime. All are willing to testify against you in a court of law."

He said, "Who can identify me and who's going to testify? If you have people, they're lying. What did Jimmy tell you . . . or was it Pernel? No, maybe it was Joseph. You're going to believe them. They're all liars and you know it."

I told him, "They didn't even say anything to me. They kept their mouths shut."

He said, "Well, you have nothing against me then."

I pulled out the picture I had to show it to him. It was the one with him, Pernel Williams, and Joseph Fuller standing near the body of the boy. I placed it in front of him. I asked, "Do you recognize anyone in the picture?"

He looked down at it. He looked up with a surprised expression. He said, "That don't mean nothing. You could have made it up."

I said, "I could have, but this is from Jimmy Dugan's collection." I pointed to each one of them and said who they were. When I finally got to him, I said, "This one here is you."

His face started to turn angry. Suddenly, he tried to lunge at me. The two agents grabbed his arms and threw him and the chair back down on the ground.

I said, "Mr. Whittaker, you have to learn to control that temper of yours, it's going to get you in a lot of trouble." I could tell he was really getting pissed off at me. I continued to tell him what I had against him. "Mr. Whittaker, I know that not only were you there when this boy was hung, but you were there when he was taken to begin with. I have eyewitnesses who will testify to that. Why don't you make life easy for you and your family and just tell me the truth and we can get this over with."

He kept staring at me. Finally, he said, "You're still going to have to prove this in a court of law, if it gets that far."

I said, "Mr. Whittaker, I hope you don't mind if I continue." He just stared at me with eyes that were seething with anger. I asked, "How many children do you have?"

He gave me an odd look. He replied, "Why do you need to know that for?"

I said, "No reason, I'm just asking. I know Pernel Williams doesn't have any. Jimmy Dugan has a baby boy and Joseph Fuller has three, two young boys and a baby girl."

He said, "All right, you want to know. I have one."

"Only one."

"Yes, only one."

I asked, "A boy or a girl?"

He said, "I have only a daughter, you know that for a fact. You saw her the day you came over to talk to me."

I said, "Oh, she was the one I saw. So she's the only one you have."

He said, "Yeah, so where are you going with this?"

I said, "I'm not going any place. I just want to make sure of my facts. What's your daughter's name?"

He said, "I'm not going to tell you."

I said to him, "Either you can tell me or I send one of my men to bring her here."

He said, "You aren't low enough to do that."

I replied, "You don't have any idea how low I'm willing to go."

He sat there for a minute or so. Finally, he said, "I'll tell you her name, only if you leave her out of this and don't tell her nothing."

I said, "I don't like making deals, but I'll make a concession this time."

He said, "Her name is Sarah Jean."

I said, "Sarah Jean, that's a pretty name."

"You better not double-cross me."

"Don't worry, I'm not going to do that."

I told the agents, "Take him back to his cell. He isn't going to be leaving anytime soon."

I had all the information I needed. Things were starting to add up and falling into place. I already knew that Andrew Whittaker murdered Nathaniel Johnson long before I even brought the four gentlemen in for questioning. I just didn't have a motive, but now I did.

I remembered when I spoke with Miss Tooley that she hadn't told me a hell of a lot, but she had said why he was murdered. Nathaniel Johnson had supposedly made a pass at a little white girl in a store. Think she said she was about ten years old and had blonde hair. I remember seeing a young girl who matched the description inside the door the day I went to talk to Andrew Whittaker. It was his daughter that Nathaniel supposedly made a pass at. I wanted to talk to his daughter, but I'd promised not to involve her.

I thought, *I have enough evidence for this to go to trial.*

I needed to go back to the field office in Atlanta and to talk to my commander. I needed to tell him that we had the man who killed the young boy and I would be able to make a good case against him with the evidence I had. Also I needed to see Agent Jones. I wanted to tell him that we found the man responsible for the young boy's death. I was hoping the information would change Agent Jones' attitude about justice in the South.

I decided to go back in the morning and leave the other agents behind. Agent Donner would be in charge while I was gone. Hopefully nothing would go wrong in my absence.

I was really happy while driving back. What once looked hopeless and bleak was now looking much better. We really needed to discuss how we were going to prosecute Andrew Whittaker—the where and how. But first things first.

I went to see Agent Jones at his home. He had been

home from the hospital for a few days after having spent a week in the hospital. I wondered how he would look. He hadn't looked too good when I left. I was sort of nervous to see him. I didn't know if he would be in good spirits to see anyone. Still, I thought once he heard what I had to tell him, he would perk up.

His house was a little outside of Atlanta, almost in the suburbs. It took me about fifteen minutes to get there. It was a nice one-story rancher set on a tree-lined street. When I walked to the front gate of the house, I saw two young children playing in the front yard—a girl and a boy. I opened the gate and walked up the cement walk that led to their front patio. The two children stopped playing and walked over to me.

The young girl asked, "Can I help you, mister?"

I said, "Not really, I'm here to see your father." I turned to the boy and put my hand out to shake and said, "You must be Franklin, Junior." He nodded his head. I turned back to the young girl and said, "You're Jamela, aren't you?" She nodded her head too. I said, "Your father has told me so much about you two."

Jamela grabbed my hand and said, "Let me take you in and see my daddy."

She took me into the house where I waited in the living room. Suddenly, Franklin's wife appeared and she ran over to me. She gave me a big hug and started to cry a little.

I said, "I hope I'm not disturbing you."

She said, "Of course not, you're always welcome in this house."

I asked her, "How's Franklin doing?"

She said, "He has his ups and downs and is still a little sore."

I asked, "Can I see him?"

146

She said, "Sure you can. I think he'd be happy to see you. He's really getting bored just sitting round the house."

She got up and walked into the bedroom. I stayed in the living room. Jamela and Franklin, Jr. just stared at me. I guess they weren't sure what to make of me.

I heard some mumbling from the back. It sounded like Franklin talking. Suddenly, he came walking out the bedroom. He was still in his pajamas. He walked very slowly across the floor. Dorothy helped him along the way. Suddenly, he turned around to her and said, "I'm not a baby, I can do it myself." She let him go and he walked very slowly towards me.

He sat down on the couch across from me. He turned to the children. "Why don't you two go out and play." At first they didn't move, then he raised his voice and told them, "Move or you'll get a spanking." They sprang up and went out the door.

I said, "I know this is a stupid question, but how are you feeling?"

He said, "You're right, that is a stupid question, how do you think I feel? I feel like shit." He laughed a little then grabbed his stomach. He said, "I feel a little better than I did when I last saw you. Anyway, it only hurts when I laugh, so don't make me laugh."

I told him, "I'll try not to do that." I started to tell him about what had happened. "I just want to let you know that we have the one that killed Nathaniel Johnson in custody." He had a surprised look on his face. I said, "Yeah, you heard what I said. You didn't think it would happen, but it has."

It seemed I had his full attention. I told him the details. "Remember that picture of all them fishing? Well, I found one of all of them that was taken the night they murdered Nathaniel. I was able to link all of them to the scene of the crime. Who would have thought a stupid picture would have done them in?"

He shook his heads and asked, "Are you sure these are the guys that did it?"

I said, "I am as sure as I'm sitting here telling you about it." I could tell he was still somewhat pessimistic. I said, "I see you're being the usual doubting Thomas."

He said, "That's only because I've been down this road before. Do you know how hard it's going to be to get this to trial?"

I said, "No. Why don't you tell me?"

He replied, "I know that you think I'm being pessimistic, but even if you get to the trial phase, it's going to be hard to get a conviction."

I said, "I think you're wrong and I'm going to prove it."

He just looked at me and shook his head. He said, "You still don't get it. Unless you're going to move the trial up north, you're going to have a hard time getting any kind of conviction."

Hearing him speak, I thought, *We can get a conviction, no matter what.*

I looked down at my watch. It was getting late and I needed to return to Miner's Bluff. There was a lot of unfinished business to take care of. I hated to leave, but things had to be done. I got up and walked over to Franklin. I put out my hand to shake.

I said to him, "I need to get back to Miner's Bluff. I have to talk to the judge down there about the other three."

He looked at me and said, "You have your work cut out for you. I hope you're right. I hope what you're saying is going to happen. You know all my thoughts and prayers are with you."

I smiled at him and left.

I had to see Judge Reynolds about getting the three arraigned and setting their bail. I had promised that if they testified against Andrew Whittaker, I would not charge them with a major crime, but only as being an accessory. Since they would be witnesses for the prosecution, they would be given immunity. Even though I didn't like it or want to do it, I needed their testimony in court if we were to convict Andrew Whittaker. Sometimes you have to dance with the devil.

I decided to wake up Judge Reynolds early in the morning. He was the only judge in the one-horse town of Miner's Bluff and mostly dealt with speeding tickets. I phoned him and it rang several times before someone answered it.

I heard a scratchy, hoarse voice speaking on the other end. "Who the hell is calling me this early in the morning? You better have a good reason."

I began to speak. "Judge Reynolds, my name is Agent Daniel Pierce. I work for the FBI. I need you to come down to the sheriff's office right away. I have some men here that need to have their bail set."

There was a long pause. He replied, "You're who and I'm doing what?" I repeated what I said. He said, "Where the hell is Sheriff Crawford? Let me talk to Sheriff Crawford."

I said, "Sheriff Crawford is indisposed at the moment. You need to talk to me."

He was not very cooperative. He was being stubborn and becoming a little irate. I'd had enough. I said, "Judge Reynolds, if you don't get your ass down here at the sheriff's office, I and two of my agents are going to come get you and drag you down here, even if you're still in your pajamas."

Suddenly, he stopped complaining. He said, "I will be there in about half an hour."

I told him, "I'll be waiting for you."

I went back to the cells where the men were. I took each one out, except for Andrew Whittaker, and told them what I was going to do. They seemed happy that they might be finally going home. I told each one that they would have to sign a confession and they would testify against Andrew Whittaker in a court of law. All said they would.

Judge Reynolds finally walked into the sheriff's office. He was a short man with gray hair, a beard, and a huge beer belly. He said, "What the hell is going on here and where is Sheriff Crawford?"

I walked over to him. I put my hand out to shake his and said, "Hello, my name is Agent Pierce. I spoke to you earlier." He just gave me a funny look.

I sat him down into a chair and said, "You see, Judge Reynolds, Sheriff Crawford has been relieved of his duties, pending our investigation."

The judge said, "What investigation are you talking about?"

I sat down beside him and told him the whole story from beginning to end. Afterwards, he just gave me a look and said, "So you expect me to make some kind of ruling on something?"

I said, "No, not exactly. I need you to set bail for the three prisoners we have in jail." I told him who they were and their crimes.

He told me, "Bring them over to the courtroom across the street from the jail."

I told my agents, "Escort all three to the courthouse. I only want Pernel Williams, Joseph Fuller, and Jimmy Dugan. I want Andrew Whittaker to stay in jail."

Nine

The judge saw them one at a time. We presented our case for the arraignment. They decided to hire the same lawyer to speak for them. I had the county solicitor speak for the government.

Judge Reynolds asked, "What are they being charged with?"

I told the county solicitor, "Don't go too hard on them. I want them to testify against Andrew Whittaker. Charge them with simple accessory to a crime." I didn't want to be more specific.

The judge heard the charges. He decided to set bail at $1,000 apiece for all of them, including Andrew Whittaker. They only needed ten percent to walk out of jail.

I thought it was a pretty low amount. They only needed $100 to get out of jail. Pernel Williams and Joseph Fuller smiled after hearing this and both said it would be no problem to get the money needed. All were allowed one phone call. Jimmy Dugan seemed the only one who was going to have problems getting the bail money.

All were going to be released from jail. I made it a point to tell them not to go anywhere and to stay in town. They didn't know it at the time, but I would have them under surveillance. I was going to watch their every move. I had a feeling that they might try to skip town.

I wanted the case moved out of Miner' Bluff. I felt Nathaniel Johnson would not receive the justice he needed there. Too many people were involved and too many people had already made a decision. Anyone we picked for the jury would probably acquit Andrew Whittaker of the charges. The town feared him. They knew if they went against him, they would pay a price. I needed the trial to be as far away as possible.

I needed someone great to argue the case, someone who had a chance of winning. It was the South, so it was going to be hard to find someone who would take it, especially because it dealt with a very explosive issue, racism. Even if we moved the trial to another town, I still had an overwhelming feeling that we might not get a fair trial or a conviction. I felt what existed in Miner's Bluff might also exist elsewhere—racism, the deep hatred that one could feel.

I went back to the field office in Atlanta. I left most of the agents in Miner's Bluff. I wanted them to keep an eye on the three who were out on bail. I was afraid they might skip town.

When I walked into the office everyone seemed happy to see me. Everyone congratulated me on solving the case. I felt good at the moment. Most of them probably thought that I would never solve the case. I walked into my commander's office.

He got up and shook my hand. He said,"Great job, Pierce. I'm really proud of you."

I should have felt good, but I didn't. Maybe it was because Agent Jones was not with me. He deserved as much praise as I did, maybe even more. He had almost died for the case.

I was still worried about the upcoming trial. I told my commander, "We need to have the trial moved to another location. I feel if we don't have it moved, everything we have fought for and have done so far will be for nothing. It will be hard to find anyone to sit on a jury who will not be tainted by who these men are. Everyone knows everyone else. These men have a hold on the town."

I decided to go to the District Attorney's office in Atlanta to see if we could do it. I was told someone who worked in the office would probably be able to help me. His name was Elwood Smith. He worked for the District Attorney's office as prosecutor for Fulton County and Atlanta. I thought he would be able to help getting the trial moved to there. I also had an alternative motive. I had heard that he tried a similar case before and won. I thought he would be our best bet for winning the case. But first things first, getting the trial out of Miner's Bluff.

His office was on the third floor of an old limestone building right across from the capital building. As I drove over from the field office, I became a little nervous. I thought, *I wonder if he will help me with the case.*

I made my way up to the third floor, by taking the steps. The building had been constructed n 1884, so there was no elevator to speak of. Thank God it was only three flights of steps.

I made my way down a long dark hallway. It was hot as hell. There was no air-conditioning or even any fans and I thought I would pass out before I reached his office.

I finally made it. It was located all he way down the hallway on the left side. I knocked on the door, but no one answered. I knocked again. Still no one answered. I decided to just walk in. I hoped the door wasn't locked. I twisted the knob, pushed the door open, and walked in.

The room was very dark. Black shades were on all the windows. I guess to keep the sunshine out of the room, so it wouldn't get hot inside. I hate to say, but it wasn't working. I looked around the room. It was cluttered with all sort of books. I decided to pick one up. I needed to dust it off. It was a law book of some sort. I opened it. Most of what I read I really didn't understand.

I walked over to the desk in the corner. Off to the side was a small metal fan. I was sweating profusely, so I decided to turn it on. I thought it might cool me off a little and stood right in front of it. There was only one speed and that was slow, extremely slow. It didn't do much good.

I stood there for a few minutes when I heard someone come in the door. I turned and saw a small figure of a man walk in and close the door. He seemed not to notice me. I decided to wait in front of the fan.

He continued towards me without looking up. He had something in his hands he was looking at it. When he was only a few feet away from me, I decided to introduce myself. "Hello, there. I hope you're Elwood Smith."

He looked up suddenly, dropping what he had in his hand. He grabbed his chest and had a startled look on his face. He said, "Who the hell are you and what the hell are you doing in my office?

I walked over to where he stood. He had bent down to pick up whatever he dropped. I said, "I apologize for frightening you." I put out my hand to shake his. I continued, "My name is Agent Daniel Pierce. I work for the FBI. I'm working on a case and I need your help."

He replied, "Well, what kind of case is it?"

I replied, "It's a murder case involving a small boy."

I looked at his reaction. He seemed somewhat interested. He started to speak with a thick southern drawl, "So what you're telling me is that a small boy murdered someone."

I said, "No, that's not what I mean." I needed to tell him the whole story and hoped he would still take the case. I said, "How can I explain this? Let me see."

I proceeded to tell him everything and he listened carefully. I asked, "Will you take it?"

He said, "Absolutely not."

I was surprised by his reaction. I asked, "Why not?"

He said, "You really want to know why I won't take this case? I'll tell you." He started to explain, "First of all, the victim is a Negro and the ones suspected are white. It is very hard to get a conviction on a white person when the victim is as Negro. Second, it's not in my jurisdiction. I can't prosecute someone if they aren't from here, but the main reason why I won't is that I don't like wasting my time on something I know will never happen."

I asked, "What's that?"

He said, "A conviction."

I thought, *Agent Jones was right.* I asked, "Maybe you could move the trial to somewhere else. Maybe to another town."

He replied, "You mean a change of venue. That's highly unlikely. Anyway, that's only if the defendant feels like he or she might not get a fair trial."

I said to him, "Couldn't that work for the plaintiff too? What if the plaintiff felt like they weren't going to get a fair trial?"

He just sat there and seemed to be thinking. Suddenly, he spoke again. "We could have the trial moved. I could put a motion in for moving at the county level, where this county is located at. But there's one problem. The plaintiff is dead. In all the years I have been doing law, I've never seen this happen."

I said to him, "There's always a first time."

He gave me strange look. He asked, "Of all the people you could have gone to, why did you pick me?"

I said, "I had information that you tried a case before like this and won."

155

He looked at me, smiled and shook his head from side to side. He said, "Yeah, you're right, I did win a case. It was about a white man that killed a Negro man. Shot him eleven times. I had him dead to rights. I had people that testified against him. I had evidence that clearly showed he did it. The jury came back in with a guilty verdict. He was sentenced to fifteen years in jail. That wasn't the end of it. His lawyer decided to appeal the verdict. I lost it on appeals. Something about a technicality. The verdict was thrown out. The defendant walked out a free man." He stopped for a second and then said, "Why do you care about this dead Negro boy anyway?"

We looked at each other. I was not going to take no for an answer. I had spent too much time on the case and was not going to let it happen. I thought about Agent Jones. I wanted to prove to him that it would not happen again. Someone had to pay for what they did

I started to speak to Mr. Smith. "So what if you lost it on appeals. This is different. We're talking about a little boy here. What does it matter whether he was black? He didn't deserve this. I spent too much of my time working on his case to simply take no for an answer. It's your duty as a human being and a prosecutor to take this case."

He seemed a little surprised by my reaction. He got up and started to walk around his office. He said, "I'm going against my better judgment, but I'll think about taking the case. I'm not making any promises. I have to see how my schedule is and if I can take this on. I'm telling you right now, it's going to be hard, so don't be surprised if nothing comes of this. Leave your number where I can reach you."

I was pleased. I got up and shook his hand very hard. I said, "Thank you so much, you don't know how much this means to me and Nathaniel Johnson's family." He just shook his head back and forth.

I walked out of his office feeling a little better. I knew it would be an uphill battle, but it had to be done. The young boy deserved better than what he got. His death had to have some meaning.

I went back to the field office and called Agent Jones. His son answered the phone.

I asked, "May I speak to your father?"

Suddenly, I heard Franklin's voice on the phone. I said, "Franklin, this is Daniel Pierce."

He didn't answer right away, then he said, "Oh, hello there, Daniel. Is there something that you want?" His demeanor sounded funny.

I asked, "Is everything all right with you?"

He paused before he answered. He started to speak, "It's my mother."

I asked, "What about your mother?"

He paused again. He started to tell me. "She died last night. It was a stroke."

I told him, "I'm sorry." I thought I should end the phone call. It would be better to tell him later about the trial.

I was about to hang up when he asked, "How's everything going with the investigation?"

I told him, "Oh, everything is going pretty good so far." I thought he was asking just to continue the conversation. I told him the details about the case and that it looked good that it would go to trial. The sound of his voice didn't change much.

I said to him, "You know, anything you need me to do, just let me know. Anything at all."

He replied, "Nothing right now, thanks for asking."

There was another pause. I decided it was time to lead the conversation. I told him, "I'll call you later. When is the viewing?"

He said, "She's going to be laid out on Friday." He gave me the address of the funeral home.

I told him, "Take care." I then hung up.

I really wanted to go to Franklin's mother's viewing. I thought I should even though I'd never met her. I really didn't know my way around Atlanta, so I asked a co-worker at the field office where the address was located. She gave me pretty good directions. I hoped not to get lost.

I made my way to the funeral home. It was not located in the better part of Atlanta. I drove down a long, poorly lit road. I drove slowly while looking at the street signs. I thought if I drove too fast I would miss the street. I finally found the street. I made a left and drove for a minute or so. I saw on the right a line of people waiting outside a small building. I saw a sign above it that said: "Moses Tubb's Funeral Home." I had found it.

I parked the car a ways down and then made my way to the funeral home. As I got closer, I saw the long line. It made its way down the street and wrapped around and down a small alleyway. I approached very slowly. I didn't know how all the black people would react to me. I was probably the only white person there. Most just gave me a strange look as I passed by. I guess they were wondering who I was and why I was there. I just kept walking without saying a thing.

I couldn't help notice how smartly they were dressed. All the women wore dresses that were black and dark blues. They wore hats with veils that covered part of their faces. The men were dressed in suits, either, black, dark blue or dark gray.

I was nearing the end of the line. A few of the people smiled as I walked past them. I tried to slip past without being noticed. As the last person in line, I looked down at my watch. It was almost 7:30.

The woman in front of me turned around and said, "My name is Annie."

I smiled and said back, "Hello, Annie. My name is Daniel."

She looked me up and down. "Don't take this the wrong way, but are you sure you're at the right viewing? This one is for a woman named Elizabeth Jones. She's a Negro."

I smiled back at her and said, "Yes, I know. Her son Franklin is a friend of mine. I never knew her, but I thought I would pay my respects to her."

She replied back, "You do. I knew Franklin when he was a just a little baby until he was eight. Then his mother decided to send him north, I think it was to Chicago."

More people started to file in behind me, so I was no longer the last one in line. I continued my conversation with Annie. I said to her, "I've only known Franklin for a short time, but I consider him a good friend of mine. You see, both I and Franklin worked with each other."

She looked at me with great surprise. She said, "You and Franklin worked together?"

I said, "Yes, but not for very long."

She then asked, "What do you and Franklin do?"

I replied back, "We work for the government. We're FBI agents."

She got a shocked look on her face. She said, "You and Franklin work for the FBI?" She started to shake her head back and forth and then turned back around.

I started to talk to her again, but she seemed to ignore me. She didn't even turn around to look at me. I thought, *What is she afraid of? I'm not going to do anything to her. I guess she has a hard time trusting white people. Maybe she doesn't trust anyone who works for the government.* I decided to just stand in line and keep my mouth shut.

I looked down at my watch again. It now read 8:15. I was

getting a little tired waiting in line, but I knew I couldn't leave now. I was only two people away from being in the front door. The line started to move again. I was finally in the front door and saw people going to the left a ways up.

I was near where the body was laid out. I peered past the corner and I saw Franklin and his wife. I saw people filing past them. Franklin looked straight down at the floor, never really looking up at anyone. People put their hand on his shoulder and tried to speak to him. He only shook his hand up and down. His wife seemed to be holding up better. She greeted and smiled at them as they walked by.

I walked past the casket and looked at his mother. She looked peaceful. She was dressed in a dark blue dress with polka dots. She had a hat on with a veil in front. She held a Bible in her hands. I bent my head down and said a little prayer for her. I made my way over to Franklin and his wife. I saw the children sitting in chairs a couple feet away from them. They seemed oblivious to what was going on.

When Franklin's wife saw me, her face seemed to light up. She put her arms out to give me a hug. I hugged her back.

She whispered in my ear, "I'm so glad you came. I didn't know if Franklin had told you. He's been very distraught about this. I know he's happy you're here."

I walked over to Franklin. I grabbed him and put my arms around him. I told him, "I'm sorry about your mother."

Suddenly, he started to weep on my shoulder. I was not ready for his reaction. I continued to hold him and let him cry. He stopped crying and put out is hand to shake mine.

He said, "Thanks for coming. You didn't have to. It means a lot."

I smiled and told him, "I needed to come. I have to leave and get back to Miner's Bluff."

He smiled, nodded his head, and said, "I understand. You have to nail their asses to the wall for what they did."

Before I left. I walked over to the children and spoke to them.

I didn't hear from Elwood Smith for about two weeks. I was waiting to hear when the trial would start and if it would to be moved to another location. I decided to call myself.

The phone rang about five times until someone picked up. It was a woman's voice.

I asked her, "Is Elwood Smith available?"

She replied, "He's not here."

I asked, "Where is he?"

She replied, "I don't know."

I became a little angry. I didn't know when I would be called back to FBI headquarters in Washington, D.C. and I wanted to be at the trial started when it started. I wanted to see the case through to the end. I decided to leave a message. I told the woman, "Tell Mr. Smith to call Agent Pierce back as soon as possible."

I waited in my hotel room for hours before I received a phone call. It was Elwood Smith.

I asked him, "Elwood, did you get the trial moved to another location?"

He said, "Agent Pierce, I'm still in the process of trying to get it moved. As I told you before, it might be a problem. I need to speak with Judge Reynolds in Miner's Bluff. It's going to be his decision to have the trial moved. If he doesn't want it moved, then it's going to be there."

I asked a few more questions. I could tell by the sound of his voice that he was not happy with my questions and that I was bothering him.

He said, "Agent Pierce, you have to understand, that is a very delicate matter. We have only circumstantial evidence and our witnesses are not of the best character. Plus we are in the south and getting a conviction on what little we have is going to be a huge task."

After listening to him, it seemed like everything Agent Jones and I had done and been through was for nothing. I replied, "I don't care what you have to do, I want someone to pay for what happened. It's your moral duty as a lawyer to see that justice prevails."

He replied, "I understand how you feel, but it's going to take some time. I need to get all my ducks in a row. I can't make any mistakes."

There was long pause while no one spoke. Suddenly, Elwood Smith said, "Agent Pierce, I really have to go now, I really have a lot to do. When I get everything where it needs to be, I'll call you and let you know everything."

Ten

It was the middle of October, over three months since the start of our investigation in June. I was back in Washington, D.C. at the FBI headquarters. I had decided to return since there was really nothing further for me to do in Miner's Bluff. Agent Jones was still recuperating at his home in Atlanta. I still hadn't received any word from Elwood Smith on how things were going. I took it as a sign that things were not going well.

I spoke to Agent Jones a few times since returning. He seemed to be in good spirits, but I can never tell with him. I thought about asking him when he was going to come back to work, but I decided not to. In fact, who knew if he was ever coming back at all. I felt lost, not knowing what would happen. My mind was back in Miner's Bluff. I couldn't help thinking about it. I wanted it all to be over. I was afraid that I would be reassigned before it happened, if it ever happened at all.

I was in my office going through some case files when the receptionist buzzed. "What is it, Charlotte?'

She replied, "Agent Pierce I have a phone call from someone named Elwood Smith. Do you want the call transferred to you?"

I didn't answer her right away. I thought, *Is this good news or bad news? If it's bad news, I really don't want to hear it.*

Charlotte repeated, "Agent Pierce, do you want this call transferred to you?"

I said, "Yes, please."

I needed a few seconds to catch my breath. I decided to speak first. "Hello, Elwood, how are you doing? I hope you're calling me to tell me some good things."

He paused for a little bit before he replied, "Well, Agent Pierce, most of it is good news."

I felt relieved. I told him, "Tell me everything."

He said, "Agent Pierce, I was able to get the trial moved out of Miner's Bluff to a town about twenty miles away called Mount Pleasant. It wasn't easy, but I was able to talk Judge Reynolds into moving it."

My demeanor changed from almost disappointment to sheer joy. I replied, "That's great, you don't know how happy that makes me."

He replied, "There's more I have to tell you. I'm still working on getting all the information I need. I need to know all the people you spoke with, whether they were black or white. I'm going to need their testimony. Some might be asked to testify for the prosecution. Also any evidence you have I'm going to need to see it, no matter how unimportant you think it might be I need all this sent to me as soon as possible."

I said, "No problem. If I have to drive it there myself, I will do it."

He said, "Just one more thing. This is still the south, even moving it to another location where no one knows about it might not help. This is going to be a tough fight. I just want you to be prepared in what you're going to see and hear. It's going to get pretty ugly."

I replied, "I'm willing to take that chance. We need this to succeed, someone has to pay one of these times."

It was now early November and the trial was to start in one day. I met with Elwood Smith, who was prosecuting the trial. He tried to be optimistic, but it would be hard case to win. We met at a small café in Mt. Pleasant. He laid out his strategy in trying the case. He decided to try to get Andrew Whittaker convicted of involuntary manslaughter. I was shocked. I felt Nathaniel Johnson had been murdered.

I told him, "I'm upset that you're not going after a murder verdict."

He told me why. "Mr. Pierce, I looked at all the evidence and the confession that you got from the others. They all said the same thing. That he was not going to kill the boy, only scare him. In all honesty, Mr. Pierce, this is our best shot, even if we get a jury of people who have not been corrupted. With the evidence and testimony we have, I might be able to get a conviction on the involuntary manslaughter."

The day of the trial arrived. It was finally going to start. Elwood Smith had been in Mt. Pleasant for a full week working on selecting a jury of Andrew Wittaker's peers for the trial. Even though the trial had been moved, I still felt any potential juror would be tainted by the way of life that was the South. *How could one be able to find a jury that would not side with Andrew Whittaker and find him innocent?* I thought.

I walked into the courtroom. It did not seem very big. Even though it was November, it seemed unusually hot. Maybe because there were so many people in the courtroom. I walked to the front of the courtroom where Elwood Smith was seated at a table on the right side. I sat down on the bench located behind him.

I bent over the railing in front of me and said very low, "Elwood, I need to speak with you."

He turned around and looked back at me. He got up and walked towards me. "I'm glad you're here, Agent Pierce." He motioned with his hand for me to sit next to him at the table, so I did.

He continued speaking to me. "Everything seems to be going accordingly. The jury has already been picked. I was able to get a mix of both men and women. Eight men and four women will make up the jury. Hopefully this trial will be over in a couple of days and we will have the verdict we want."

I smiled and said, "I certainly hope so."

I went back to where I was sitting. The courtroom started to fill up. More and more people were crowding into the room. I looked at each person who entered. None were Agent Jones.

I bent forward again towards Elwood Smith and said, "Elwood, I don't see Agent Jones anywhere. He's got to be here to testify."

Elwood turned around and pointed towards the back and upwards. He said, "Right there is where he's at."

I turned and looked around. There was a balcony that went around the top of the courtroom. I saw Agent Jones there. I didn't understand why he was up there.

I turned back around and asked Elwood, "Why is he up there?"

He said, "Agent Pierce, this is the South. Whites and Negroes do not sit together."

I turned back around and waved for him to come down. He put his hand up and moved it from side to side while shaking his head back and forth. He was saying, "No."

I watched as the people poured into the courtroom. I saw the family members of all the people involved in Nathaniel Johnson's killing enter and sit behind the defendant's table. They did not look very happy. Then, one by one, the defendants, Pernel Williams, Joseph Fuller, and Jimmy Dugan were led into the courtroom. They all sat together in the front row behind the defendant's table.

Suddenly, the courtroom door swung open and there

stood a very tall and somewhat fat elderly gentleman. I guessed he was the one defending Andrew Whittaker. He walked down the aisle and over to the left side of the courtroom, where the defendants were, and sat down at the table. He threw a big case he was carrying on the table. He opened it and then started to take papers out of it. He looked at them as they were laid out on top of the table.

I heard a loud voice come from the back of the courtroom. The door swung open. It was Andrew Whittaker. He didn't seem to be in a very good mood. He was arguing with the bailiff the entire time he walked down the aisle. He looked over at me and smiled. He then walked and sat next to the gentleman at the table.

Elwood Smith turned around and motioned me to come closer. He said, "Andrew Whittaker has a good lawyer. That's Henry Lloyd Jenkins. He the best damn defense attorney money can buy. I wonder how someone like Mr. Whittaker can afford someone like him."

I said, "You're not worried, are you?"

He replied, "A little, he's a pretty smart lawyer and can charm the birds out of the tree." He was not making me feel very confident.

The jury was seated. There were eight men and four women. They all looked to be over sixty years old. Some of the men wore overalls; all the women wore dressess. They all had a look on their faces like they didn't want to be there. The judge walked in and sat down behind the huge desk.

Elwood turned around and said, "Judge Frederick Richardson is going to preside over this trial. I heard he's pretty liberal in his thinking. Hopefully he will be here."

Elwood Smith was to give his opening statement first. He got up from the table and walked towards the jury box. He stopped and looked at each one of them. He then stepped back a little and started.

"Ladies, and gentlemen of the jury, the case I will be presenting to you is like no other before. This is not simply a case of a young Negro boy's death, but a way of thinking and, yes, even a way of life where intolerance, bigotry and hatred is the prevailing attitude. Where a simple gesture can get you murdered. I will prove to you that Andrew Whittaker, the defendant, willfully and maliciously and with a callous attitude, caused the death of Nathaniel Johnson and the evidence that I will present will prove this."

It was Andrew Whittaker's lawyer's turn next. He got up and walked over to the jury and smiled at them. Then he quickly turned and stared at Elwood Smith and started his opening statement while pointing his finger at him.

"Ladies and gentlemen of the the jury, Mr. Smith, the prosecutor, talks about this as not just a trial about a boy's death, but about a way of life. What way of life is he talking about? Is he talking about how my client got up every morning and went to work and provided for his family? Is he talking about how he loved and took care of his children? Is he talking about how we go to church every Sunday? What's he really talking about? This is not about a way of life, but how my client is being railroaded into something that he had nothing to do with. How a bunch of government goons came down here to our fine town and harassed our good people. How they fabricated evidence. The real evidence will prove my client had nothing to do with it." He finished and walked back to his side of the courtroom, sneering at Elwood.

Elwood Smith called his first witness, Reverend Jackson. He got up from the balcony and made his way down. He walked slowly down the aisle to the front of the courtroom. All eyes were on him. One could almost feel the hatred in the courtroom as he made his way to the witness stand.

The bailiff went over to him. He put out a Bible and said, "Please raise your right hand and place your left hand on the Bible. Do you swear to the truth, the whole truth and nothing but the truth, so help you God?"

Reverend Jackson answered with a simple, "Yes."

Mr. Smith walked over to Reverand Jackson and then started his questioning. "Reverend Jackson, what is your full name?"

The reverend had a troubled look on his face. He answered back, "My full name is Otis Matthew Jasckon."

"And where do you live?" Mr. Smith asked.

Reverend Jackson gave his address and the town where he lived. I didn't unerstand the line of questioning.

Mr. Smith then asked, "Reverend Jackson, can you tell me what you saw on the night of February 12, 1963?"

Reverend Jackson paused for a moment and then he started to speak. "I saw four men grabbing a young Negro boy, throwing him into their car."

Mr. Smith asked, "Can you describe the car?"

Reverend Jackson replied, "It was either a burgundy or maroon-colored statinon wagon."

"Did you happen to see the license number?" asked Mr. Smith. Reverend Jackson told him the number.

Elwood went back to his table. He picked up a plastic bag and a document. He handed the judge the item and asked, "With the court's permission, this will be considered 'Exhibit A' in this case."

He then awalked over to Henry Jenkins and showed it to him. He looked at what was in the plastic bag and the document. It was the vehicle identification plate from the car I had found in the woods and the document was from the Motor Vehicle Department stating who owned it.

He objected and said, "Your Honor, this car is not my client's and it has no bearing on this case."

Mr. Smith countered, "He was in this car when the boy was killed, so it can be presented as evidence."

The judge overruled Andrew Whittaker's lawyer's objection.

Elwood Smith continued questioning Reverend Jackson. "Mr. Jackson, can you now point out the person or persons you saw in the vehicle?" He pointed directly at Andrew Whittaker. Elwood Smith asked, "Are you sure that's the man you saw?"

Reverend Jackson replied, "That's him, that's who I saw drag Nathaniel Johnson into the car."

Elwood Smith said, "Your Honor, I don't have anymore questions at this time to ask Mr. Jackson."

Andrew Whittaker's lawyer rose and walked over to Reverend Jackson. He stopped right in front of him and smiled. He began to question him. "Mr. Jackson, you said my client was the one you saw drag Nathaniel Johnson into the car."

Reverend Jackson said, "Yes, I saw him."

He continued. "How can you be so sure it was my client and not someone else? Maybe it was Pernel Williams or maybe it was Joseph Fuller. How can you be sure it was my client?"

Reverend Jackson answered back, "I know what I saw and I know that was him."

Henry Jenkins continued questioning Reverend Jackson. "Mr. Jackson, how old are you?"

Reverend Jackson replied, "I'm sixty-five years old."

Henry Jenkins then asked, "Mr. Jackson, being sixty-five, don't you think that your eyesight might not be what it once was?"

Reverend Jackson replied, "My eyesight is just fine and I know what I saw that night. I saw four men get out of a car and take Nathniel Johnson and one was Andrew Whittaker."

Henry Jenkins asked, "If you knew these persons did this, why didn't you go to the police?"

Reverend smiled and paused for a moment, then he

spoke. "Mr. Jenkins, I find it hard to believe you would ask me that question, but I'll tell you why. First of all, I'm a black man living in the South. Do you really think if I went to the police that they would have believed me and then done something about it? That's a stupid statement to make, don't you think?"

There was an audible gasp in the courtroom.

Henry Jenkins was angered by what Reverend Jackson said. He retorted, "Mr. Jackson, you as a black man have just as much rights as I do and any white man has down here in the South and what you have said has offended me. I plead with you, Judge Richardson, to hold this man in contempt of court."

Judge Richardson smiled and said, "If you don't get on with this questioning, I'm going to hold you in contempt."

Henry Jenkins put his hand in his vest pockets and walked back to the defendant's table in a huff. Reverened Jackson looked up at the judge and smiled.

Henry Jenkins came back to Reverend Jackson. He asked, "I'll ask you again, why didn't you go and tell the police?"

He answered, "I told you why, they would not have believed me."

Henry Jenkins tried a different approach, "Mr. Jackson, why didn't you tell someone else, someone you thought might listen to you? Someone that might have done something?"

Reverend Jackson replied, "Like who? Who was I going to tell? Tell me who else was I going to tell."

Henry Jenkins answered, "Mr. Jackson, are you telling me there was no one you could have gone and told this to?"

Reverend Jackson said, "There was nobody."

Henry Jenkins walked back and muttered, "I just don't

believe it." He then turned around and said to the judge, "I have no further questions at this time."

The judge asked Elwood Smith, "Do you want to question Reverend Jackson again?"

He answered, "Yes, I would."

Elwood Smith got up and walked over to Reverend Jackson and asked, "You said you didn't go to the police because you didn't feel that they would believe you and also they would not have done anything about it. Do you believe in your heart that this is true?"

Reverend Jackson replied, "Abolutely."

Elwood Smith walked back to the table and picked up what appeared to be letters. He then handed them to Reverend Jackson. He asked, "Do you know what these are?"

Reverend Jackson replied, "Yes, they are letters that I have received ever since that night I saw Andrew Whittaker and those other three that're sitting over there take Nathaniel Johnson."

Elwood asked, "Could you tell me what's in the letters?"

He replied, "All of them say that if I tell anyone or go to the police and tell them what I saw, they would kill me and any family member of mine."

He then gave the letters to Andrew Whittaker's lawyer to look at. He shuffled through them, looking at each one, and then gave them back to Elmwood Smith.

Elwood went back to the table and grabbed another piece of paper. It was a letter I had found in Pernel Williams' house. He handed it to Henry Jenkins and said, "The one who wrote all those letters is the same one who wrote this letter in my hand. It was Andrew Whittaker."

Henry Jenkins looked back at Andrew Whittaker, who just shook his head and said, "No."

Elwood continued with his questioning, "Reverend Jackson, has everything you said to the court been true?"

Reverend Jackson replied, "It's God's honest truth."

Elwood asked, "Why should we believe you?"

Without batting an eye, Reverend Jackson anwered back, "Mr. Smith, I'm a man of God. I speak and teach the gospel every day. I know that one day I'm going to meet my maker and I know that I will have to have a clear conscience when I do. I could never lie about anything."

Elwood Smith said, "I have no further questions."

The judge asked Henry Jenkins, "Do you want to cross-examine him?"

He simply said, "No."

Elwood called me to the stand. I knew he would eventually, but I was still a little nervous. Elwood started his questioning.

He asked me, "What's your name and what do you do for a living?"

I told him and the people in the court, "I am an FBI agent."

He asked, "Why are you here in Georgia?"

I told him, "I was investigasting the death of Nathaniel Johnson."

He asked, me, "Why do you think Andrew Whittaker is the one who murdered Nathaniel Johnson?"

I said, "All the evidence we have gathered up to now points to him. The confessions that we obtained from Pernel Williams, Joseph Fuller, and James Dugan were conducted separately and all said the same. That Andrew Whittaker was the one that killed Nathaniel Johnson."

Elwood Smith paused for a moment, then he asked, "You believe those three in what they told you?"

I said, "Absolutely, They all said the same thing, word for word. Why would all three make up the same story? They didn't have time to get together and do it."

Elwood Smith told the judge, "I don't have any more questions to ask him."

Judge Richardson asked, "Henry, do you have any questons to ask him?"

He replied, "I certainly do. Mr. Pierce, it's your claim that my client was the one that murdered Nathaniel Johnson."

I replied, "Yes, without a doubt."

Henry Jenkin paused for moment and came back at me. He said, "Are you telling me at no time you never suspected anyone else other than my client, even though there were three other people in the car that could have committed this crime?"

I retorted, "We looked at all the evidence. It pointed to one person and that was Andrew Whittaker."

Henry Jenkins asked me, "Give me one piece of evidence that makes Andrew Whittaker the murderer."

I said, "The only reason that Nathaniel Johnson was murdered was because he spoke to this little girl. This little girl was about ten years old and had blonde hair. The only person of the four who has a daughter of that age and hair color is Andrew Whittaker and if you don't believe me, why don't you ask him."

Henry Jenkins turned and looked over at Andrew Whittaker, who had bowed his head. He said, "I have no further questions at this time."

Judge Richardson asked, "Elwood, do you have any more witnesses?"

He said, "Yes. Will Elizabeth Tooley take the stand?"

I believe if it hadn't been for the woman and her ignorance, we wouldn't be sitting there. She walked slowly to the stand.

Elwood started questioning her. "Miss Tooley, do you recognize the defendant?"

She put on her glasses that hung around her neck. "No, I don't recognize him."

Elwood replied, "So, it's my understanding that you don't know who he is?"

She said, "That's what I said." She seemed to be somewhat annoyed.

Elwood continued. "Didn't you tell Agent Pierce, who is sitting over there that Nathaniel Johnson had made a pass at a young blonde white girl in the store?"

She put her glasses back on and looked over at me. She replied, "I don't recognize him."

Elwood said, "So what you're telling me that Agent Pierce is a liar when he told me that you told him why Nathaniel was murdered."

She replied, "My memory isn't what it used to be. I get mixed up a lot."

Elwood retorted, "I'm sure you do, Miss Tooley."

I could tell Elwood Smith was somewhat angry with Miss Tooley. He continued his questioning in a harsher tone. "Isn't it true, Miss Tooley, that you were in the store that day? You saw that young black boy talking to that little white girl and it made you angry?"

She snapped back, "I know your kind. You're tring to put words into my mouth."

Elwood kept at her. "Isn't it true that you were the one that told her mother of what you saw and that's what started this whole thing? Isn't it true that he was just talking to her and that made you angry? That this little Negro boy had the nerve to talk to that little girl?"

Henry Jenkins jumped up from his seat and said, "Your Honor, I strongly object. Mr. Smith is badgering the witness. He's making Miss Tooley look like she should be on trial."

Judge Richardson said, "Objection sustained, Mr.

Smith, please watch your line of questioning. I don't want to have to reprimand you again."

Elwood apologized for his outburst and then said, "Your Honor, I have no more questions for Miss Tooley."

Judge Richardson asked Henry Jenkins, "Do you have any questions to ask?"

He replied, "Not at this time."

I bent forward to where Elwood Smith sat. I asked him, "Why don't you put Pernel Williams on the stand or any one of them? Their testimony will back us up."

Elwood turned around and said, "I would love to, but I'm afraid they would rescind their testimony and lie on the stand. I'd rather not chance that and if I don't put them on the stand, neither will Henry Jenkins. He doesn't want to take the chance that they would actually testify in our favor."

Elwood Smith went over to the bailiff and whispered something in his ear. I wondered what he had said. The bailiff simply nodded and then walked down the aisle and out the courtroom door. About a minute later he walked back in through the door with Andrew Whittaker's daughter.

As they walked down the aisle to the front of the courtroom, she smiled and waved at people. The look on Andrew Whittaker's face told everyone that he was not happy. As she walked past him, she waved at him and said, "Daddy, I love you."

Right then Andrew Whittaker got up and yelled at me, "You promised you weren't going to involve her. You lied, you bastard!" His laywer had to restrain him.

I walked over to where Elwood Smith stood and called him over to me. He came over and asked, "What do you want?"

I said, "What the hell are you doing? I told you that I promised not to get his daughter involved."

He retorted, "You may have promised, but I didn't.

Weren't you the one that told me to do anything to get a conviction? Well, I'm doing that."

The bailiff walked over to Andrew Whittaker's daughter. He told her, "Put your hand on the Bible and swear to tell the truth."

She did so with one hand while the other played with her hair. He told her to sit down. She giggled the whole time.

Elwood Smith walked over and started to talk to her. He tried to be delicate because he didn't want to upset her. He asked, "What is your name?"

She replied, "My name is Sarah Jean Whittaker."

He asked her, "Where do you live and how old are you?"

She answered his questions with a slightly nervous giggle.

He then asked her, "Who's your father?"

She said, "That's my daddy sitting over there." She pointed in the direction of the defense's table. Everyone could see the anguish on Andrew Whittaker's face.

Elwood Smith continued questioning. "Sarah Jean, I'm going to ask you a few more questions. Is that all right with you?"

She nodded her head. He walked over to the table and started to go through all the paperwork on it. He pulled out a picture of Nathaniel Johnson and walked back to Sarah Jean.

He handed the picture to Sarah Jean. She looked down at it and then up and smiled at Elwood Smith.

Elwood asked her, "Have you ever seen him before?"

She said, "He looks like the colored boy that was talking to me that day in the store. When my Daddy found out that he talked to me, he was mad."

He reiterated to her, "Are you sure this is the boy that talked to you that day in the store?"

177

She nodded her head and said, "Yes."

Elwood asked, "Do you know what his name was?"

She said, "I think he said his name was Nathaniel."

Elwood then got very close to Sarah Jean, put his hand on her shoulder, and said, "You're not lying to me, are you?"

She replied, "No, I'm telling you the truth. My daddy said if I ever lied to him he would beat me to an inch of my life and that I would go to hell."

Elwood asked her, "You said your daddy was mad when he found out that the boy talked to you. What did he say to you?"

Andrew Whittaker's attorney stood up and said, "Your Honor, I object. My distinguished colleague is trying to put words in her mouth."

The judged replied, "Objection overruled. He's simply asking her a question. I don't see that he's putting words in her mouth."

Elwood continued his questioning. "Sarah Jean, you said your daddy was mad. Was he real mad?"

She replied, "Oh, he was terribly mad. He yelled at me really loud. His face was all red. He scared me and made me cry."

Elwood asked, "Sarah Jean, do you see anyone else in this courtroom that you saw that day?"

He looked from one side of the room to the other several times. She stopped, looked up at Elwood, and said, "Yes, I saw that lady over there."

I turned around. She appeared to be pointing towards Miss Tooley. Elwood walked back to where Miss Tooley was sitting and said, "Did you mean this woman?"

She smiled and said, "Yeah, she's the lady I saw."

Elwood Smith walked back to Sarah Jean and said, "Thank you, Sarah Jean, you did really good."

She smiled back and then looked at her father, who just looked down at the table.

Elwood walked back to the table, turned around, and said, "I don't have any more questions, Your Honor."

The judge asked if the defense attorney had anything to ask her. He stood and simply said, "No, Your Honor."

It was time for the closing arguments. Elwood Smith went first. He got up from the table and walked over to the jury box. He looked straight at the jury.

He began to speak, "Ladies and gentlemen of the jury, now comes the hard part. It's time for you as jurors to make your decision on the guilt or innocence of the defendant. I tried to make my case for a guilty verdict. I have presented you with eyewitness testimony from friends who said what Andrew Whittaker's intentions were—to scare Nathaniel. He might not have meant to kill Nathaniel Johnson, but his action that night did cause his death. Even his daughter corroborated what his intentions were." He stopped and said, "Excuse me, please."

Elwood walked over to the table, drank some water, and then cleared his throat. He walked back over to the jury box. I guess his mouth was dry and he needed a drink before continuing.

He started again. "Nathaniel Johnson needed not to die. He was murdered simply because of what he was. He was Negro. That's right, a Negro. His only crime was his skin color."

He stopped again and walked over near Andrew Whittaker. He pointed his finger towards him and started again, "And this man played God. Who gave him that right? There is only one God and we all have to answer to him. He has no right to decide on who has the right to live and the right to die. If you are religious and God-fearing people, which I know you are, you will hand down a verdict of guilty.

179

Because no one has the right to make that decision. Not me, not you, not the judge, not even Andrew Whittaker. Only our maker has the right. I know in my heart of hearts that you all know this to be true. Remember, when it's your time to meet the Almighty God, you better have a clear conscience when you do. Nathaniel Johnson deserves better than what he got. He was the victm in all of this." Elwood then fnished simply with, "God bless all you and God bless America."

It was Andrew Whittaker's lawyer's turn to give his closing statement. He walked over to the jury box, looking smug and with his hands in his vest pockets. He started, "Ladies and gentlemen, my fine colleagues would like you to believe that my client had something to do with the death of that boy. He said what he did led to the death of the boy, that what he did caused his death. Isn't it strange that this is based on confessions that were given by my client's so-called friends? Funny they all said that my client caused the death of that boy. All these men were there in the car with my client, but somehow they escaped being prosecuted for giving their testimony against my client. Strange, don't you think?"

He continued, "Mr. Smith claims that if you believe in a higher power, you should come back with a guilty verdict. That's strange, I thought as as jury you would make your decision on the evidence presented to you, not on if you are God-fearing people. Ladies and gentlemen, none of the evidence that has been presented makes my client guilty of murder in this case. I asked you to base your decision on the facts and not feeling. Thank you all and may God bless you."

There was silence in the courtroom. Henry Jenkins walked back to the table and sat next to Andrew Whittaker. I looked at the jury. I had a bad feeling. I thought, *Even with all the evidence and testimony we had, will these people find Andrew Whittaker guilty or is what Agent Jones said, that a person of color is doomed to a horrible existence as long as they live here in the South, true?*

The judge explained the process by which the jury had to come to a decision. They listened very carefully as he spoke. He the told the jury, "Go back to the jury room and do not come back until you make a decision."

As I watched them leave, it was hard to tell what they were thinking. I knew if their decision took a long time, it would appear favorable to the prosecution. If they came back in half an hour. I knew we had probably lost the case.

Elwood Smith got up and walked back towards me. He said, "It's all in their hands now. I tried my best, but you never know if that's good enough down here in the South."

I grabbed his hand to shake it. I told him, "You did all you could. What more could you have done?"

Both of us walked out of the courtroom together. As we went down the steps of the courtroom, he said, "I'm going back to my hotel room until they come back with a decision."

I said, "I'm hungry. I think I will go over to the small restaurant they have in town."

My meal had just been put in front of me when a young boy ran into the restsurant. He shouted out my name so I waved to him.

He came over to me and asked, "Are you Daniel Pierce?"

I said, "Yes, I'm Daniel Pierce."

He replied, "I have a message from a Mr. Elwood Smith, he says, 'You better get back to the courthouse now.' "

I swallowed the food in my mouth, pulled out a ten-dollar bill to pay my check, and ran out of the restaurant back to the courthouse. I had a bad feeling as I ran. It had only been forty minutes since the jury had left the court-room.

I rushed up the steps of the courthouse and made my way to the courtroom. I walked down the aisle and sat behind

Elwood Smith. He turned around and motioned me to come close, so I did.

He said, "I don't have a good feeling about this. It was such a short deliberation I don't think this is going to work in our favor."

To tell the truth, I had a sick feeling in the pit of my stomach too.

Suddenly, the judge came in from a door off to the side. He sat behind his desk and then motioned the bailiff to bring the jury back in. The jurors walked single file back into the jury box. None looked at Elwood Smith or Andrew Whittaker. They all looked down towards the ground. None seem very happy.

The judge said, "Will the foreman of the jury please stand." An elderly gentleman with all white hair stood up. Then the judge asked, "Has the jury reached a verdict?"

The foreman of the jury said, "Yep."

The judge asked, "What say you the jury in this case?"

The foreman paused for what seemed a long time. At that moment I had a gut feeling that everything we had done was for nothing.

Suddenly, he began to speak. "We the jury find the defendant Andrew Whittaker . . ." He paused again. Then he began to speak again. He repeated himelf, "We the jury find the defendant Andrew Whittaker . . . we find the defendant Andrew Whittaker guilty of involuntary manslaughter."

I couldn't believe my ears. I thought I heard the word "guilty." Suddenly, all hell broke out in the courtroom. Some people began yelling at the jury, at the judge, and at us. I saw Andrew Whittaker's wife crying and then Sarah Jean started to cry. The sheriff started to lead him out of the courtroom. Sarah Jean ran to him and grabbed him around his waist. The bailff had to pull her away. It was a very sad scene.

As Andrew was being led out. I heard his lawyer say to

him, "Don't worry, this isn't over. I'm going to appeal this as soon as I can. They haven't won this case yet."

I went over to where Elwood Smith was standing. I smiled then grabbed a hold of him and gave him a big hug. I was very happy with the outcome. Elwood Smith grabbed my hand and shook it. He didn't seem as happy as I was.

He said, "Henry Jenkins is right, this isn't over yet. This verdict can always be overturned. So enjoy it while you can." He then walked by me and out the courtroom door.

I turned around and looked up at the balcony to find Agent Jones. I didn't see him there, so I made my way out of the courtroom.

As I came down the courthouse steps, a lot of black people approached me. They grabbed my hand and thanked me for what I had done.

Reverend Jackson came over to me and said, "It was a great day when you and Agent Jones came down here. You stood up for us for our cause and I will never forger that."

I smiled and shook his hand. I kept looking for Agent Jones as I made my way through the crowd. Finally I saw him near a car. His wife was standing by him.

I walked over to him and said, "I told you I wouldn't let you down. I know it isn't going to make up for all the other things that have happened down here, but it's a start."

Agent Jones replied, "I hope you're right, but I have a feeling this is going to be short-lived. Things don't always seem what they look to be."

I said, "Franklin, you will always be the eternal optimist to me. Don't ever change." I asked him, "Are you going back to headquarters in Washington?"

He said, "I don't really know, I'm still thinking about it."

"I hope you do." I shook his hand and told him, "I really hope you don't leave. You're a great agent, and the agency needs great agents."

He and his wife got in their car. I bent down and kissed his wife good-bye. He drove away and I waved as his car disappeared down the road. My time in Georgia had finally come to an end. I can't say that I will miss being here.

It's November 22, 1963 and I've been sent to Dallas to do surveillance around the motorcade route. Nothing really interesting, just going to observe. Agent Jones decided not to come back to the FBI. It's a pity because he would have made a great agent. But I guess we will never know, will we?